Unicorn Princesses

SUNBEAM'S SHINE
FLASH'S DASH
BLOOM'S BALL

Unicorn Princesses

SUNBEAM'S SHINE
FLASH'S DASH
BLOOM'S BALL

Emily Bliss

illustrated by Sydney Hanson

BLOOMSBURY

NEW YORK LONDON OXFORD NEW DELHI SYDNEY

Sunbeam's Shine, *Flash's Dash*, and *Bloom's Ball* first published in the
United States of America in 2017 by Bloomsbury Children's Books
Bind-up published in the United States of America in December 2017
www.bloomsbury.com

Bloomsbury is a registered trademark of Bloomsbury Publishing Plc

For information about permission to reproduce selections from this book, write to
Permissions, Bloomsbury Children's Books, 1385 Broadway, New York, NY 10018
Bloomsbury books may be purchased for business or promotional use.
For information on bulk purchases please contact Macmillan Corporate and
Premium Sales Department at specialmarkets@macmillan.com

Library of Congress Catalog-in-Publishing Data
for each title is available upon request
Sunbeam's Shine LCCN: 2016036842
Flash's Dash LCCN: 2016036844
Bloom's Ball LCCN: 2017010910

ISBN 978-1-68119-935-1 (bind-up)

Book design by Jessie Gang
Typeset by Westchester Publishing Services
Printed and bound in the U.S.A. by Berryville Graphics Inc., Berryville, Virginia
2 4 6 8 10 9 7 5 3 1

All papers used by Bloomsbury Publishing, Inc., are natural, recyclable products
made from wood grown in well-managed forests. The manufacturing processes
conform to the environmental regulations of the country of origin.

For Phoenix and Lynx

Unicorn Princesses

Princesses

SUNBEAM'S SHINE

Chapter One

In the top tower of Spiral Palace, a green wizard-lizard waved his wand at an orange ear of corn. He took a deep breath. And then he chanted, "Alakazam! Alakazoop! Unicorn, unicorn! Alakaboop!" He waited for the ear of corn to turn bright pink. But instead, the lights flickered and the walls shook. Thunder rumbled and boomed. Blue and green lightning flashed across the sky, which had grown dark as night.

"Oh dear! Oh dear!" the wizard-lizard cried out. "Did I say 'unicorn, unicorn'? I meant 'ear of corn, ear of corn'! Oh dear!" The wizard-lizard turned pale green. He frantically waved his wand at the ear of corn and yelled, "Undo! Undo! Cancel that spell! Delete! Erase! I take that one back!"

But the palace lights kept flickering. The thunder rumbled even louder. Yellow and silver lightning flashed.

"Oh, not again!" the wizard-lizard exclaimed. "The unicorn princesses are going to be so angry this time. They told me to stop casting spells on vegetables." He raced over to the window just as a glittering yellow sapphire rose up into the sky. Then, with one final burst of thunder, the brightly colored stone dropped into a shimmering, purple canyon in the distance.

"That was Princess Sunbeam's magic gemstone," the wizard-lizard said, covering his face with his scaly hands. "Without it, Sunbeam doesn't have any magic powers. Now I've really done it!"

The wizard-lizard leaped over to a box in the corner of the room. He pulled out a book, looked at the cover, and tossed it aside. He pulled out another book and threw it. And then another. Finally, he found the right book. In silver letters, the title read, *The Book of Unspells*. The wizard-lizard leafed through the pages, muttering, "Oh dear, oh dear! Princess Sunbeam has lost her magic, and it's all my fault!"

He read out loud from a page at the back of the book, "There is only one way to reverse a spell that robs a unicorn princess of her magic gemstone. A human girl who believes in unicorns must travel to the Rainbow Realm, find the lost gemstone, and return it to the princess. Only then will the princess regain her magic powers. Note: Only human girls who believe in unicorns are able to see them." The wizard-lizard's eyes filled with excitement.

"We need a human girl! And one who can see unicorns!" he cried out as he raced from the room and down the palace's spiral staircase to find the unicorn princesses.

Chapter Two

One Saturday afternoon, Cressida Jenkins was on a hike in the woods with her family. Her parents walked up ahead, and her older brother Corey followed just behind them. He looked through a pair of binoculars. "I see a hawk!" he called out. "Oh, wait. It's just another crow."

What Cressida really wanted to see,

much more than a crow, or even a hawk, was a unicorn. Her parents had told her many times unicorns weren't real. "They're imaginary, honey," her mother would say. Cressida always nodded, but she couldn't help but wonder if her mother might be wrong.

Real or imaginary, if there was one thing Cressida loved, it was unicorns. Posters of pink and purple unicorns covered her bedroom walls. She had a unicorn bedspread, unicorn curtains, and a unicorn lamp on her bedside table. Her pink book bag had a picture of a unicorn on the back. She even had unicorn pencil erasers for school and silver unicorn sneakers with pink lights that blinked when she walked, jumped, and ran. In art class, she had painted six unicorn watercolor pictures. They all hung on the refrigerator next to the week's school-lunch menu and Cressida and Corey's soccer game schedules.

Cressida's father turned around right in front of the biggest oak tree Cressida had ever seen. "It's time to head back," he said. "We need to get home in time to go to the grocery store before dinner." Cressida sighed. She didn't want to go home yet, even if the only birds were crows and there were no unicorns. Plus, she hated going to the grocery store. No matter what Cressida said or did, her parents wouldn't buy Frosted Marshmallow Unicorn-Os cereal. The box was pink and shiny with a picture of a gigantic purple unicorn leaping from a cereal bowl. "It's too sugary," her father always said as he pushed the cart right past the Unicorn-Os. Then he usually pulled a boring, brown box of Whole Wheat Squares off the shelf.

As Cressida turned to follow her parents and Corey back to their house, she looked down at her sneakers and jumped. The blinking pink lights always cheered her up.

Just then, Cressida glimpsed something shimmering in a pile of leaves near the gigantic oak tree. She stepped to the side of the path, reached down, and picked it up. It was a long, old-fashioned key. But the strangest part about it was the handle, a sparkling, pink crystal ball.

"Honey," Cressida's mother called out. "Did you find something?"

"Just an old key," Cressida said. And she slipped it into her pocket.

👑

That evening as she got ready for bed, Cressida pulled her favorite green unicorn pajamas from her dresser drawer. As she started to take off her jeans, she felt something heavy and pointy. She stuck her hand into her pocket and wrapped her fingers around the key. She had forgotten all about it!

As Cressida cupped the key in her hands, she noticed the crystal ball on the handle now glowed emerald green. Had she imagined the ball was pink that afternoon?

"Huh," she said. She put the key on her dresser, next to a unicorn statue she had made from pipe cleaners and milk cartons.

When Cressida's mother came to tuck her in, she saw the key. "What a strange key!" her mother said. "It's beautiful!"

"When I found it, the handle was pink," Cressida said.

"That's odd," her mother said. Cressida could tell from her mother's voice she didn't believe her. It was the same tone she used when she told Cressida that unicorns were imaginary. "It was probably just the sunset reflecting on the glass."

"Hmm," Cressida said, but the more she thought about it, the surer she felt the handle had been pink.

Chapter Three

As soon as Cressida woke the next morning, she jumped out of bed and grabbed the key off her dresser. Now the crystal ball was blue, the color of the ocean! Was her mother right that the light made the ball look different colors? Cressida opened her curtains and switched on her unicorn lamp. But even in the crisp, clear morning sunlight, the ball glowed dark blue.

She stared at the key for a long time. Did it fit into the gate of a secret, magic garden? Or unlock a treasure chest? Or open a castle door? Maybe it belonged to a

fairy or a witch or even a troll. And then she whispered out loud, "What if whoever dropped this key in the woods goes back to look for it? What if they need it and are trying to find it?"

Cressida suddenly felt guilty she had taken it. Maybe she should have left it there, in the pile of leaves. She decided she should return it as soon as possible.

She quickly put on her favorite outfit: black jeans, a green dress with a unicorn on the front, bright yellow socks, and her blinking unicorn sneakers. She left a note for her parents saying she went for a walk and would be home in time for breakfast. And then she raced out the door, through her backyard, and into the woods where her family had walked the day before. Cressida sprinted along the forest path, her sneakers blinking, until she got to the giant oak tree.

Cressida kneeled down and reached into her pocket for the key. She decided to leave it sitting on a root of the oak tree instead of under the pile of leaves where she found it. That way, it would be easier to see.

Just then, Cressida heard a rustling noise behind her. And then a high voice, unlike any she had ever heard, said, "Oh, I know I left it here. I know I did. Where is it? I'll never get home!"

Cressida sucked in her breath. The voice didn't sound like it belonged to a human.

She turned around slowly. And then she froze. Cressida couldn't believe her eyes. Right in front of her, five feet away, was what looked like a yellow pony. Its coat was the color of a buttercup, and it had gold hooves, a silky blond mane, and—a shiny gold horn! It wasn't a pony, Cressida realized as she drew in her breath. It was a unicorn!

Cressida pinched herself. The unicorn was still there.

She closed her eyes, counted to five, and opened them again. The unicorn was still there.

She pinched herself so hard she whispered, "Ouch!" The unicorn was *still* there.

Cressida watched, her mouth open and

her eyes wide, as the unicorn rummaged through the leaves with her nose and hooves. A necklace made of blue ribbon hung around the unicorn's neck. Cressida noticed a large hole in the ribbon, and she wondered if something that had been attached to the necklace was missing.

"Oh, where is it?" the unicorn said again.

"Are you looking for this?" Cressida asked, holding the key out in front of her. Now the ball glowed pink again.

The unicorn reared up and stepped backward. With large, dark eyes she looked down at the key. An enormous grin spread across her face. "The key!" she whinnied. "Thank you!" Then, with

her mouth, she took the key from Cressida's hand. Cressida's heart skipped a beat. A unicorn's nose had just brushed against her skin.

♔

Then the unicorn froze. She looked at Cressida, narrowed her eyes, and dropped the key between her hooves. "Wait a minute!" the unicorn said. "Can you see me?"

"Of course," Cressida said. It seemed like an awfully strange question.

"Are you absolutely sure?" The unicorn flicked her blond mane and twitched her blond tail.

"Of course I'm sure!" Cressida said, laughing. "You're standing right in front of me. You just touched my hand with your nose."

"You can see me! You can see me!" the unicorn sang out, dancing in a circle and rearing up on her hind legs. "You're a human girl who believes in unicorns!"

"Well," Cressida said, giggling, "yes, I suppose that's true."

"You must come back with me to the Rainbow Realm," the unicorn cried. "Please say you will! And by the way, my name is Princess Sunbeam."

"Back to where?" Cressida asked. "And you're a princess? Should I curtsy?"

"Don't bother curtsying," Sunbeam laughed. "The Rainbow Realm is a magic land ruled by my sisters and me. Usually, we stay away from the human world, but I have a little bit of a problem. Well, actually a big problem. And I really need your help."

"What's wrong?" Cressida asked. She tried to imagine what kind of problem a royal unicorn could have.

"I bet you noticed that hole in my necklace," Sunbeam said, crossing her eyes and looking down toward her chest.

Sunbeam's face looked funny, but Cressida managed to nod instead of laugh.

"My magic yellow sapphire, which gives me my special power, is gone. Without it, I might as well be a pony with a golden horn!" Sunbeam exclaimed dramatically.

Now Cressida couldn't help but giggle. When she caught her breath, she asked, "How did you lose your yellow sapphire?"

Sunbeam sighed. "Well, there's this wizard-lizard—his name is Ernest—who lives in our palace. And when he gets bored, he amuses himself by casting spells on the fruits and vegetables. Usually he tries to turn them different colors, just for fun, but sometimes he tries to change them into spiders and butterflies. We've asked him to stop because his spells always go wrong. Always. But he never listens. And so this time, he accidentally cast a spell that made my yellow sapphire fly off. Now it's lost, and the only way to reverse the spell is for a human girl who believes in unicorns to find my magic gemstone and return it to my necklace. Ever since yesterday morning, I've been in your world, walking right up to human girls. And they've stared through me, like I'm made of air. That's because they don't believe in unicorns. You're the first one who has been able to see me. I'd given up, and I was ready to go home. And then I found you while I was looking for my key."

Cressida smiled with delight. "My mother keeps telling me unicorns are imaginary. But I've always known unicorns are real."

"My mother used to tell me humans smell funny," Sunbeam said, pushing her nose toward Cressida and inhaling loudly. Cressida suddenly wished she had taken a bath that morning. After several seconds of sniffing, Sunbeam said, "My mother was wrong! You don't smell bad at all."

Cressida giggled with relief.

"So," Sunbeam said, "will you come back to the Rainbow Realm and help me find my magic gemstone?"

Cressida's heart swelled with excitement. And then she remembered her parents, who would worry if she wasn't home soon. "The only thing," she said, "is I left my parents a note saying I'd be back in time for breakfast."

"No problem," said Sunbeam. "Human time will freeze while you're in the Rainbow Realm. When you come back out, it will be exactly the same time as when you came in. You'll be back in plenty of time for breakfast."

"Well," Cressida said as her heart

thundered in her chest. She couldn't remember ever feeling so excited and nervous. "What are we waiting for?"

Sunbeam reared up and whinnied with excitement. "Fantastic!" she said, and then she lowered down onto her knees. "Climb onto my back."

"I've never ridden a unicorn, or even a pony," Cressida said.

"Well, I've never been ridden before," Sunbeam said. "Hold on to my mane, and we'll figure it out together."

Carefully, Cressida climbed onto Sunbeam. The unicorn's back was warm, soft, and surprisingly steady. Her mane felt like threads of silk in Cressida's hands. Sunbeam stood, picked up the key with her mouth,

and trotted over to the oak tree. Then she pushed the key into a tiny hole Cressida had never noticed in the tree trunk. Suddenly, the forest began to spin. It whirled faster and faster, until the trees were just a green and brown blur. Cressida gripped Sunbeam's mane as tightly as she could.

And then she had the feeling the two of them were falling. It was like being in an elevator hurtling downward without stopping at any floors.

With a jolt, the spinning and falling stopped. Cressida blinked. They were in one of the biggest, grandest rooms Cressida had ever seen. Purple velvet curtains hung from floor-to-ceiling windows. Crystal chandeliers sent rainbow light all over the white marble floors. Along one wall were silver troughs filled with water and something else that looked, Cressida thought, like honey or maple syrup. Harp music played softly, and silver candles burned in glass holders.

"Welcome to Spiral Palace," Sunbeam said.

Chapter Four

Sunbeam kneeled, and Cressida slid sideways off Sunbeam's back. Her sneakers' pink blinking lights reflected on the shiny white floor. She closed her eyes and breathed in. The air smelled like pine trees and lavender.

"Get ready to meet the other unicorn princesses," Sunbeam whispered. She winked at Cressida before she called out,

"Hey, everyone! I'm back! And guess what I found?"

Cressida heard the sharp clatter of hooves against the marble tiles. And then six more unicorns, each a different color and each wearing a gemstone necklace, were standing in the room.

"These are my older sisters," Sunbeam said to Cressida. "The silver one is Princess Flash. Her magic power is to run so fast lightning bolts shoot from her horn and hooves. The green one is Princess Bloom. Her magic power is to make things grow and shrink. The purple one is Princess Prism. She paints beautifully and can change the color of any object. The blue

one is Princess Breeze. She can make the strongest gusts of wind you can imagine. The black one is Princess Moon. Her power is to make everything dark as night. And the orange one is Princess Firefly. She can create swarms of fireflies and make things glow."

The unicorn princesses swished their tails and flicked their manes as they stared at Cressida with wide, unblinking eyes.

"It's wonderful to meet you," said Cressida. "I'm Cressida Jenkins. I'm not a princess. I don't have any magic powers. But I sure am excited to be here." Cressida curtsied just for fun. She couldn't imagine another time she might have the occasion to curtsy in front of a herd of unicorn princesses.

Flash stepped forward with a serious expression on her face. A diamond, attached to a pink ribbon around her neck, shimmered in the light of the chandelier. "Are you absolutely and positively sure you see us?" she asked.

"Yes," Cressida said.

Flash sniffed several times. Then she turned to Sunbeam and whispered, just loud enough that Cressida could hear, "Isn't it odd that she doesn't smell? I was expecting to have to open some windows and turn on a fan."

Sunbeam whispered back, "I know. I

thought I'd have to hold my nose the whole time I was in the human world. But it turns out humans don't really smell. At least, most of them don't."

"Interesting," Flash whispered, and then the two sisters looked at Cressida. Cressida pretended she hadn't heard them as she tried not to giggle. She decided not to mention that human boys, especially her brother, often smelled terrible.

"Cressida," Flash said, "has Sunbeam explained to you her situation with the wizard-lizard and the magic spell?"

"Yes," Cressida said. She wanted to ask if she would get to meet the wizard-lizard, too. She was curious to find out what, exactly, a wizard-lizard looked like. But when she saw Flash's icy eyes, she decided to ask Sunbeam about the wizard-lizard later.

"Did Sunbeam tell you about the different domains inside the Rainbow Realm?"

"The domains?" Cressida said. "I don't think so."

Flash frowned.

"I was getting to that," Sunbeam said. And then she whispered to Cressida, "Flash is the oldest sister. Nothing I do is ever good enough for her." Cressida nodded in sympathy. She knew exactly what it felt like to be a younger sister.

"Well, allow me to explain," Flash said in a tone Cressida associated with her teachers at school.

Sunbeam rolled her eyes and snorted.

Flash sighed and continued, "Our mother, Queen Mercury, divided up the Rainbow Realm so that each princess could have our own land, or domain, to rule over. She decided which princess would get which domain based on our magic powers. Since Sunbeam's power is to create heat and sun, she rules over the Glitter Canyon. Our best guess is that Sunbeam's yellow sapphire is in the canyon. I know it's a lot to take in all at once. Does that make sense to you?"

Cressida nodded to show she understood.

"Are you sure?" Flash asked. "I can explain it all again."

"I've got it," Cressida said. She wondered if Flash thought human girls weren't very smart. Perhaps Queen Mercury had told her daughters that humans were both smelly and dumb.

"Very well," Flash said. "Are you willing to go to the Glitter Canyon this morning to look for Sunbeam's yellow sapphire?"

"Absolutely," Cressida said. She felt a surge of excitement. She had never been to a canyon before, and certainly not one that glittered.

"Splendid," Flash said, and she smiled. "Have you had breakfast?"

Cressida suddenly realized she was very hungry. She hadn't eaten since dinner the night before. "Not yet," she said.

Flash used her mouth to pick up and ring a silver bell. Almost as soon as it made a soft tinkling noise, five scarlet dragons, each wearing an apron and a chef's hat, whistled as they walked in pushing gold troughs on wheels. Threads of blue smoke and tiny green flames danced from their nostrils.

"Thank you," Flash said.

"No problem," one of the dragons said as green fire erupted from his mouth.

"Dragons are great cooks," Sunbeam whispered into Cressida's ear. "They don't even need stoves or ovens because they breathe fire. And they can cut our fruit using their claws instead of knives."

Cressida nodded as she watched the

dragons leave the room, their red tails dragging along the floor. "I had no idea dragons were real, too," she said.

"Of course they are," said Sunbeam, shrugging. "Anyway, I'm starving. Let's have some breakfast."

Inside the troughs were what looked like slices of purple-and-pink striped tomatoes with teal seeds alongside piles of what looked like cookies made with hay and orange berries instead of oatmeal and raisins. The unicorns dipped their mouths into the troughs and began to noisily chew. Cressida watched, unsure of what to do. Was she supposed to get on her hands and knees and eat from the trough, just like the unicorns? To her relief, one of the dragons returned with a silver platter piled high with striped fruits.

"Thank you so much," Cressida said, taking the tray.

Cressida's stomach growled as she bit into the fruit. It was the freshest, juiciest fruit she had ever had. She decided it tasted like a cross between a kiwi, a fresh peach, and a coconut. The little blue seeds were crunchy and sweet, like toffee.

"What is the name of this fruit?" Cressida asked Sunbeam. "It's amazing!"

"Those are giant roinkleberries from

Bloom's garden. She's an amazing gardener! She uses her magic power to make the fruit grow and the weeds shrink."

Bloom nodded as she chewed a roinkleberry. The emerald on her necklace glittered. "It's a good thing I can use magic to grow my fruits and vegetables. Now that Sunbeam's yellow sapphire is gone, there's no sun for my garden."

"Now that I've found Cressida, that should change soon enough," Sunbeam said. "I'm sure she'll find my yellow sapphire in no time."

"I'll do my very best," Cressida said. She felt a little nervous. What if she couldn't find the gemstone? "I can do this," Cressida whispered to herself. And then she took a deep breath and ate another bite of her roinkleberry. After she felt full— roinkleberries were quite filling—she slipped a roinkleberry in her jeans pocket, just in case she felt hungry later.

As soon as the unicorns finished eating, Sunbeam jumped up, full of energy. "Well, let's go!" she said. "I can't wait to show you Glitter Canyon." Then Sunbeam whispered to Cressida, "And I'm ready for a break from Flash. I love her, but my oldest sister drives me crazy sometimes!"

Cressida smiled. "I know the feeling. I have an older brother."

Sunbeam kneeled down, and Cressida climbed onto her back.

"Good-bye!" Sunbeam called to her

sisters, trotting in an excited circle. "The next time you see me, I'll have my yellow sapphire and my magic powers back."

Sunbeam swished her tail and, with Cressida still perched on her back, trotted toward the palace door. "Good luck!" the unicorn princesses called out after them.

"Sunbeam," Flash called out, "no fooling around. You and Cressida have serious work to do!"

Chapter Five

Outside the glass door, Sunbeam trotted along a path of clear, shining stones that led away from the castle and toward a thick pine forest. For a moment, Cressida turned and looked behind her at Spiral Palace. She knew, right then, how it had gotten its name: the princesses' home was shaped

* * *

like a giant, white, glittering unicorn horn, and spiraled up toward the sky. "Wow," Cressida whispered.

As soon as they were out of sight of the palace, Sunbeam ran faster and reared up, laughing as she jumped and played. "Whoa!" Cressida yelled, wrapping her arms around Sunbeam's neck. But she couldn't help giggling as Sunbeam danced in circles.

"Don't let Flash get to you," Sunbeam said. "She's way too serious. There's plenty of time to have fun today, even while we're searching for my yellow sapphire." The princess sped up and leaped over a pine tree that had fallen across the path. "I'm just excited to be out of that hot, stuffy palace with that silly harp music and those smelly candles." Sunbeam whinnied as she jumped over several more fallen trees. Then she began to gallop, and for several minutes Sunbeam raced along a narrow, winding forest path. Finally, she slowed down. "We're almost to the Glitter Canyon!" she announced.

Sure enough, the forest was getting thinner, with fewer and fewer trees. "Close your eyes!" Sunbeam called out. "I can't wait for you to see the canyon! You're going to love it!"

Cressida shut her eyes. She felt Sunbeam speed up, and she tightened her grip on the unicorn's mane. Suddenly, the air felt much cooler, as though Sunbeam had just walked into a refrigerator. Cressida shivered.

"Okay! Now you can look!" Sunbeam called out, her voice high with excitement. Cressida opened her eyes and sucked in her breath. She and Sunbeam stood on the edge of a beautiful purple canyon. At the top were towers of gigantic plum-colored rocks, patches of lavender grass, fields of violets, and pebbles that looked like silvery grapes. Down at the bottom of the canyon were clusters of cacti in every shade of purple Cressida could imagine, and sand that looked just like the purple glitter she used in art class at school. Cressida had never seen so much purple in her life!

"Welcome to the Glitter Canyon!"

Sunbeam sang. "It's my very own part of the Rainbow Realm!" Sunbeam kneeled down, and Cressida slid off her back.

"This is incredible," Cressida said. "It's the most beautiful place I've ever seen."

"It's even more beautiful when the sun is in the sky," Sunbeam said, sighing. "And it's much, much warmer. You'll be amazed by how gorgeous it looks once you find my yellow sapphire and I can make the sun come out."

That's when Cressida noticed there was something strange about the light in the canyon. The purple sand didn't shine, even though it looked like glitter. The cacti didn't have any shadows. And the light seemed dim, as though it were a cloudy day, even though the sky was completely clear. Cressida looked up at the sky. The sun was missing! No wonder it was so cold. Cressida shivered and rubbed her arms. She wished she had brought her winter coat.

Just then, Sunbeam ran forward, danced in a circle, and said, "Come on! Let's go down to the bottom of the canyon. We can start looking for the yellow sapphire there."

Cressida and Sunbeam walked together along a path that led to the bottom of the canyon. Lizards, turtles, and frogs the color of grape jelly climbed and hopped on the towers of rocks, and light purple parakeets perched in the branches of silvery purple trees.

As they hiked, Cressida felt a sudden

burst of heat. And then something small and red scampered across the path and disappeared behind a rock. At first, Cressida thought it was a chipmunk. But when it crossed the path again, this time closer to Cressida and Sunbeam, Cressida could see it looked just like a red and orange candle flame with flailing arms, legs, and a tail.

"Yikes!" Cressida called out. "What is that?"

"Oh, that's a flame-bite," Sunbeam said. "Just make sure it doesn't touch you. And make sure you don't drop any roinkle-berry seeds on the ground. Flame-bites love roinkleberry seeds so much they'll follow you around for days hoping you'll feed them."

The flame-bite darted behind a bush with plum-colored leaves. And then it scampered out, right in front of Cressida and Sunbeam. It shrieked and scurried in circles, so its arms, legs, and tail danced in every direction. Cressida jumped backward. She shielded her eyes from the flame-bite's bright light. Beads of sweat formed on her forehead from the flame-bite's heat.

"Shoo!" Sunbeam said. "Go away!" The flame-bite screeched and ran away. "They're not dangerous, but they sure are annoying," Sunbeam said. "At least they go away as soon as you tell them to." As soon as the flame-bite left, the cold returned. Cressida shivered and hoped the bottom of the canyon would be warmer.

Chapter Six

By the time Sunbeam and Cressida hiked to the bottom of the canyon, Cressida was so cold her teeth were chattering.

"It's pretty chilly," Cressida said, touching her arms, which were covered in goose bumps. "You don't have a coat I could wear, do you?"

"Hmm," Sunbeam said. "Unicorns

don't really wear coats, so I don't have one for you to borrow. Some of my sisters like to wear capes, but the Glitter Canyon is usually so hot that I don't have one. Not that it would fit you anyway."

Just then, out of the corner of her eye, Cressida saw something the color of egg yolks amid all the purple. She turned and there, hanging on a lavender cactus, was a furry yellow jacket and yellow boots with a fuzzy lining. Both were exactly the color of Sunbeam.

"Look at that!" Cressida said. She and Sunbeam walked over. On the jacket hung a sign that said, **Dear Cressida, Thank you for your help. Sincerely, Ernest.**

"Ernest?" Cressida said, hurriedly

putting on the coat. "That's the wizard-lizard, right?"

"Yes," Sunbeam said. "I bet he meant to make the coat and boots purple, and they came out yellow." They both giggled.

Cressida took off her blinking unicorn sneakers and put on the yellow boots. "How do I look?" she asked. She twirled around in a circle.

"Fabulously yellow!" Sunbeam exclaimed. "But still not quite as yellow as I am."

Cressida felt much warmer now that she had her coat and boots.

"Well," she said, eyeing the rocks and sand and cacti. "I guess we better start searching for your sapphire. Where have you already looked?"

Sunbeam blushed and glanced down at her hooves. "The truth is I haven't started. I just don't even know where to begin. It could be anywhere."

Cressida nodded. She looked at the stretch of purple sand in front of them.

And the mounds of purple rocks. And the clusters of purple cacti. There must have been millions of cracks, crannies, and crevices where a yellow sapphire could be hiding. She could see exactly what Sunbeam meant. It was hard to decide where to begin. Cressida took a deep breath. She knew from doing school assignments that the only way to finish a big project was to do a little bit at a time.

"Let's start by searching down here, at the bottom of the canyon. Why don't you go over there and use your hooves to look through the sand?" Cressida pointed to a stretch of sand next to several scraggly purple pine trees. "And I'll go over here and sift through the sand with my hands."

Cressida pointed to a stretch of sand on the other end of the canyon, next to several cacti.

"Sounds good!" Sunbeam said. She trotted over to the pine trees and began to dig with her hooves and nose.

Cressida walked over to the cacti and sat down in the purple sand. It felt cold through her jeans, and she was grateful that the wizard-lizard had thought to make a warm coat and boots magically appear. Cressida grabbed a handful of sand and let it slide through her fingers. Then she grabbed another handful. And another.

Just then, she thought she heard a noise that sounded like chuckling. She stopped and looked around. She didn't see anyone.

Maybe it was the desert wind, Cressida thought. She shrugged and grabbed another handful of sand. She heard the laugh again. But this time the same voice said, "Oh golly! Oh gee! That tickles!"

Cressida looked all around her. That time she was sure it wasn't the wind. Then she noticed the ground shaking slightly. Cressida grabbed one more handful of sand. The laugh was even louder, and the ground trembled even more. "Oh golly golly gee!" the voice cried out. "That tickles!"

"Who's there?" Cressida asked. She wondered if some magic canyon creature was hiding behind a cactus.

"It's Danny," the voice said. "Danny the Dune."

"Danny the Dune?" Cressida asked. "Where are you?"

Danny the Dune laughed. "You're sitting on me," he said. Cressida looked down. All she saw was purple sand. And then the sand beneath her trembled, and the laughter grew even louder. Suddenly, the ground underneath her rose up, so she was sitting atop a small hill. Right below her legs, two big violet eyes opened and a purple mouth curled into a smile.

"Tricked ya, didn't I?" Danny said. "I bet you didn't know you were sitting on a dune!"

Cressida giggled with delight. "What's a dune?"

"It's a sand hill. You've probably seen us

at the beach. Or maybe the last time you visited the desert." Cressida didn't have the heart to tell Danny the Dune she had never been to the desert. And she'd only been to the beach once, when she was five. She didn't remember it well enough to know if she'd seen any sand dunes. "A few of us dunes live here, at the bottom of the Glitter Canyon."

"I'm sorry I keep tickling you," Cressida said. "I'm looking for Sunbeam's yellow sapphire. Have you or any of the other dunes seen it?"

Danny made a strange growling noise. "Well," he said. "I heard from Denise, who heard from Darryl, who heard from Doris, who heard from the twins, Dave and Devin, that the cacti have the yellow sapphire. They're hiding it from everyone. On purpose." Cressida figured that Denise, Darryl, Doris, Dave, and Devin were all dunes.

"The cacti?" Cressida said. "Do the cacti talk, too?"

"Well," Danny said, sounding even angrier, "the cacti *can* talk. And they used to talk to us all day long. But after we told them to give the yellow sapphire back to Sunbeam, they told us they didn't have it. And then they stopped talking to us. It's awfully lonely down here in the canyon without any cacti to talk to."

"Hmm," Cressida said. She could hear not just anger, but also hurt in Danny's voice. He sounded like he missed his friends. And she also got the feeling there was more to the story than what Danny had told her. "Would you mind if I tried to talk to the cacti?" she asked.

"Be my guest," Danny said. "Maybe they'll tell you where they're hiding the yellow sapphire."

Chapter Seven

Cressida stood up and brushed sand off her coat, her jeans, and her boots. Just like glitter, the sand stuck to everything.

Cressida tiptoed over Danny, trying not to tickle him with her feet, though he chuckled each time she pressed her boot into the ground. She climbed over a pile of rocks that looked like giant eggplants, and stopped in front of a shivering purple cactus with its arms folded tightly across its chest.

"Hello there," Cressida said, and she smiled her kindest, friendliest smile.

The cactus blinked and frowned. Its teeth were chattering and its lips had a bluish tinge.

"I know you're really cold," Cressida said, "but would you be willing to talk to me just for a moment?"

"It depends," the cactus snarled. "Did the dunes send you up here?"

"No," Cressida said. "I've come on my own. My name is Cressida Jenkins. Princess Sunbeam brought me here to find the yellow sapphire."

The cactus stared at Cressida for a long

time and sighed. "I'm Corrine," she finally said. She unfolded one of her arms, smiled, and reached a prickly hand out toward Cressida. After a few seconds, Cressida realized the cactus wanted to shake her hand. Careful to avoid Corrine's needles, Cressida used her thumb and index finger to take the cactus's hand. "With a name like Cressida, you could be a cactus," Corrine said. "All our names begin with *C*."

"I'd love to be a cactus like you," Cressida said, trying to be polite. But truthfully, Cressida thought being a cactus sounded terrible. She would hate to be rooted to one place in the ground, even if it meant living with unicorn princesses in the Rainbow Realm.

"I'm relieved you've come to find Sunbeam's yellow sapphire," Corrine said. "We're all freezing cold. And we can't just put on a coat the way you can."

"That sounds awful," Cressida said. "I'll find the sapphire as soon as I possibly can. And that's why I came to talk to you. Do you have any ideas about where I should look?"

"The dunes are hiding the sapphire on purpose," Corrine sniffed. "Though you'll have to be the one to ask them where it is. The cacti aren't speaking to them."

"Why aren't you speaking to them?" Cressida asked. She wanted to hear the other side of the story.

"Well," Corrine said, crossing her prickly

arms even more tightly, "they kept accusing us of hiding the yellow sapphire on purpose. When we told them for the hundredth time that we don't have it, the dunes called us liars. And then they said our needles are dull and our flowers are ugly. That's when we quit talking to them." Cressida thought the fight between the dunes and the cacti sounded like the arguments she had with her brother Corey.

"I see," said Cressida. She wanted to be careful not to take sides. "Wait, did you say you have flowers?" Cressida asked, looking more carefully at the cacti. She didn't see a single flower.

With one of her arms, Corrine pointed to several green lumps on her head and chest. "These are our flowers. We can only open them in the sun," Corrine explained. "As soon as the wizard-lizard cast his spell, all our flowers shut."

Cressida looked at the three other shivering cacti standing near Corrine. Sure enough, they were all covered in the same green lumps.

"What color are your flowers?" Cressida asked. She imagined the cacti looked brilliant in the sunlight, with their flowers open.

"Mine are magenta," Corrine said proudly.

"Mine are blue," another cactus said. "I'm Claude, and it's a pleasure to meet you."

"Mine are pink," said another. "I'm Carl."

"Mine are yellow," said one more, who, Cressida noticed, looked worried. "I'm Callie."

"It's a pleasure to meet all of you. And I bet your flowers are beautiful," Cressida said. "I promise I'll find Sunbeam's gemstone as soon as I can."

"Thank you," the cacti said in unison.

"Have any of you actually seen the yellow sapphire?" Cressida asked.

"Of course not," Corrine, Claude, and Carl replied in unison. Cressida noticed Callie said nothing. Instead she cast her eyes downward and frowned nervously. Cressida thought Callie looked like she had a secret, and Cressida wondered if that secret was about the yellow sapphire.

Cressida walked over to Callie and leaned in as close to Callie's ear as she could without getting prickled. "Callie?" she whispered. "Can I ask you a question?"

Callie tightened her shivering arms. She looked so worried Cressida thought she might start crying. Cressida wanted to give her a hug, but that didn't seem like a good idea, given the long, sharp purple needles that covered Callie's body.

"I'm wondering if you know anything about where the yellow sapphire could be," Cressida whispered.

"What are you two whispering about?" Corrine called out. Callie's eyes widened.

"Nothing!" Cressida called back. And then to Callie she whispered, "Any secrets you have are safe with me."

"Do you promise not to tell Corrine, Claude, and Carl?" Callie whispered.

"I promise not to tell anyone anything without your permission," Cressida answered.

Callie took a deep breath and blinked back several tears. "Well, on the day Ernest cast the spell, it was very strange here in the Glitter Canyon. There was thunder and lightning. The sky got dark. And then the sun vanished. Just then, I felt something hard and heavy land in one of my flowers. At first I thought it was one of the purple rocks that are all over the canyon. But just before my petals shut, I caught a glimpse of something yellow and glittery. I'm almost positive the sapphire is inside one of my closed flowers, but I can't open it without the sun." Callie took a deep breath. "I'm afraid to tell the other cacti because they're so sure the dunes have the yellow sapphire. And I'm afraid to tell the dunes because they're already so angry at us. I've been afraid to tell Sunbeam because she's the princess, and I don't want her to get mad at me."

Cressida felt thrilled she had almost surely found the yellow sapphire, but concerned for Callie. "Thank you so much for trusting me," Cressida whispered. "Don't worry. We'll find a way to get the sapphire out of your flower. But I do think I'd better tell Sunbeam."

"Do you think she'll be angry?" Callie asked.

"I don't know for sure," Cressida said, "but I doubt it. And even if she is, I bet you two will be able to work it out."

"Well," Callie said. She bit her lip and furrowed her brow. "Okay. You can tell Princess Sunbeam."

"Thank you," Cressida said. And with that, she ran across the canyon as fast as she could, all the way back to Sunbeam.

"Sunbeam!" she cried out, breathless. "Guess what?"

Sunbeam dropped a long purple stick from her mouth and raised her head. Cressida glanced down at the sand by the unicorn's hooves and saw that Sunbeam had been drawing pictures of suns, rainbows, and girls riding unicorns. "My eyes were so tired from looking at the purple sand that I was worried that even if the yellow sapphire was right in front of me, I wouldn't see it. I decided to take a break," Sunbeam explained. "Did you find it?"

"I know where it is," Cressida said, and she told Sunbeam about her conversation with Callie.

"Good job," Sunbeam said. "I knew a girl who believes in unicorns could find it." The unicorn furrowed her brow. "Now we just have to figure out how we can get the yellow sapphire out of Callie's flower. Without the sun, she can't open it."

"Hmm." Cressida had hoped Sunbeam would have an idea.

Just then, a flame-bite scampered in front

of Sunbeam and Cressida. For a moment it stood still, and Cressida squinted and shielded her eyes from the flame-bite's bright light. After only a few seconds, she felt as though she had stepped into a hot oven, and she unzipped her yellow coat. Suddenly, the flame-bite squealed and scurried in circles around Sunbeam, flailing its arms and legs as it ruined her drawings.

"Shoo!" Sunbeam said, stamping her hoof. The flame-bite shrieked one last time and dashed behind a violet-colored pine tree. Immediately, the cold returned.

"Rats!" Sunbeam said. "That silly flame-bite ruined the best picture I've ever drawn of a human girl. Before I met you, I always thought humans had tails."

Cressida laughed. And then, as she zipped back up her coat, she had an idea. "Sunbeam," she said slowly, "how high can flame-bites jump?"

"They can't jump at all," Sunbeam said. "They just run around and shriek."

"And you said they like roinkleberry seeds?" Cressida asked.

"They love roinkleberry seeds. They'll do almost anything to get them."

Cressida pulled the roinkleberry from her pocket, split it in half, picked a teal seed from the center, and threw it as far away from them as she could.

"Good throw," Sunbeam said, admiring how far the seed had sailed.

For a few seconds, the seed lay in the

sand. Then a flame-bite scurried from a pile of rocks and popped the seed into its mouth. As soon as it finished chewing, it screeched and ran in circles, searching for more.

"Watch out," Sunbeam said. "If it thinks you'll feed it, it will follow us everywhere." Fortunately, the flame-bite didn't realize Cressida had thrown the seed, and it darted back behind the rocks.

"I've got a plan!" Cressida exclaimed, jumping up and down. "But we'll have to get the cacti and the dunes to work together."

Sunbeam swished her tail and frowned. "I doubt that will work," she said. "They've had arguments before, but I've never seen them this angry."

"I know they're angry," Cressida said, thoughtfully, "but I think it's possible they can be friends again. Every time my friends and I have gotten into an argument, we've found a way to talk about it and make up. If they didn't still care about each other, they wouldn't feel so angry and hurt."

Sunbeam raised one yellow eyebrow and shrugged. "I guess we can try!" she said. "What should we do first?"

"Hmm," Cressida said. "The first step is to go talk to Callie."

"Climb on!" Sunbeam kneeled, and Cressida quickly climbed onto the unicorn's back.

Chapter Eight

Sunbeam galloped across the Glitter Canyon, her gold hooves kicking up a cloud of purple dust behind them. As the cold wind rifled through Cressida's hair, she closed her eyes and smiled. There was nothing in the world better than riding a unicorn, she decided.

Sunbeam stopped on the other side of

the canyon, right in front of Corrine, Claude, Carl, and Callie.

Callie glanced at Cressida with a look of panic. Cressida smiled reassuringly at the nervous cactus, slid off Sunbeam's back, walked over to Callie, and leaned as close to Callie's ear as she could. "I have an idea for how to get your flower to open," Cressida whispered, "but we'll need the dunes to help us. Could I have your permission to tell the other cacti and the dunes what happened?"

Callie took a deep breath and said, with a wavering voice, "If we need to tell everyone, I'd like to do it myself."

"That's very brave," Cressida replied.

Callie took another deep breath. She looked at Corrine, Claude, and Carl. And then she looked down at the six purple sand dunes—Danny, Denise, Darryl, Doris, Dave, and Devin. "I have something important to say," she announced.

The other cacti, who were whispering among themselves, stopped their conversations and looked up. But the dunes frowned, closed their eyes, and began to slide away. Then Danny yelled, "We're not talking to the cacti until they admit they're holding the yellow sapphire on purpose!"

"We don't have it! You do!" Claude snarled back. "You're just jealous that we have flowers and you don't. You're

hiding it on purpose so we can't open our flowers."

"That's ridiculous," Darryl snorted. "You're just jealous that we can slide around and you're rooted to the ground."

Soon, all the cacti and all the dunes were screaming. Cressida covered her ears. Sunbeam whinnied and reared up, trying to get everyone to be quiet, but the cacti and the dunes only yelled louder.

Cressida bent down, plucked a blade of purple grass, put it between her thumbs, and blew as hard as she could. The grass made a high whistling noise. Finally, all the cacti and all the dunes fell silent.

"As ruler of the Glitter Canyon, I command you to listen while Callie speaks,"

Sunbeam said. The dunes closed their sandy purple mouths. The cacti shut their bluish-purple, prickly lips. Sunbeam looked at Callie. "Go ahead," she said.

"Well," Callie said, "I think the yellow sapphire is stuck in one of my flowers."

Doris muttered, "I knew it!"

Callie continued, "I promise I haven't been holding it there on purpose. It landed there when the wizard-lizard cast his spell. And then my flower closed, and I couldn't open it. I was afraid to say anything because I didn't want to make the fight between the dunes and the cacti worse. I'm sorry for not telling you sooner. I didn't know what to do."

The dunes grumbled among themselves, but Cressida could tell they felt less angry. They could hear in Callie's voice that she was telling the truth: she wasn't hiding the yellow sapphire on purpose, and she wanted to get it out of her flower—and back on Sunbeam's necklace—as quickly as possible.

Finally, Danny said, "We're sorry we said all those mean things to you. We just felt frustrated."

"And cold," said Darryl. "I'm always mean and cranky when I'm cold."

Corrine laughed. "Me too," she said.

"Yes, me too," Claude and Carl added.

There was a long silence, and Cressida held her breath.

Danny cleared his throat. "Friends again?" he asked.

"Yes, friends again," Corrine said.

When all the dunes and all the cacti smiled and cheered, Cressida exhaled. She felt a warm, full feeling in her heart.

"I feel much better now," Callie said. Then she looked at Cressida. "But I'm still really cold. Didn't you say you have a plan to get my flower to open?"

"I sure do," Cressida said. "For my plan to work, we all have to work together. Are you ready?"

They all nodded.

"Great," Cressida said. "First, I need all the dunes to get in a circle around Callie and to lie as flat as possible." The dunes looked puzzled, but they slid over to Callie and arranged themselves in a tight circle.

They flattened and closed their eyes and mouths.

"Perfect!" Cressida said. "When I yell, 'Up!' I need you to get as tall as possible, so tall that you're like a wall around Callie. And I need you to stay like that until I yell, 'Got it!' Can you do that?"

"Yes," Danny, Denise, Darryl, Doris, Dave, and Devin all said in unison.

"Fantastic," Cressida said. Then she looked at Sunbeam. "Would you mind standing right here?" Cressida pointed to the sand behind Danny. "If it's okay with you, I'll need to sit on your back."

"Sure," Sunbeam said, looking confused as she walked over to Danny.

Cressida winked at Sunbeam and

smiled reassuringly at Callie. And then she pulled the roinkleberry from her pocket and picked out a handful of seeds. She placed a seed on Danny's forehead, and another one a few inches away on his nose. She kept putting down roinkleberry seeds until she had made a trail leading across Danny and right up to Callie. Then, in front of Callie's closed flower, she left a pile of seeds.

Cressida ran over to Sunbeam, climbed onto her back, and whispered, "Now we just have to wait."

Soon enough, a flame-bite, running and shrieking, found the first seed Cressida had placed on the ground. It crouched down, popped the seed into its mouth, and then moved on to the next seed, and then the next, moving closer and closer to Callie. When it found the pile of seeds right in front of Callie, it began cramming them into its mouth.

"Up!" Cressida called out.

The dunes rose up as high as they could, surrounding Callie and the flame-bite with a high, sandy wall. In the flame-bite's heat and light, Cressida noticed Callie's flower had started to open just a little bit. Her plan was working!

When the flame-bite gobbled up the last of the seeds, it began to shriek and run in circles, trying to get away. But the dunes were too steep, and it was trapped right in front of Callie. Cressida watched as Callie's flower kept slowly opening.

The dunes panted and grunted. "How much longer?" Dave and Devin groaned.

Cressida looked at Callie's flower. It was halfway open. "You're doing an amazing job!" she yelled. "Just a little longer! You can do it!"

The flame-bite screeched even more frantically. Cressida pushed her hand into her pocket, and, to her relief, she found several more seeds that had fallen out of the roinkleberry. She tossed them right in front of Callie, and the flame-bite stuffed them greedily into its mouth. Callie's flower opened a little more. And then a little more. Now Cressida could see the yellow sapphire. "If I climb up on your neck, could you please get me as close to Callie's flower as possible?" Cressida asked Sunbeam.

"Of course," Sunbeam said, and she craned her neck toward Callie.

Meanwhile, Danny cried, "I don't think I can stay like this much longer!"

"You can do it! We're almost there!" Cressida exclaimed. She slid onto Sunbeam's neck and leaned forward. Then she reached her left arm toward the yellow sapphire. But when she tried to grab it, her fingertips barely brushed the gemstone. She wasn't quite close enough.

"Hold on tight!" Sunbeam whispered.

Then, with a whinny, Sunbeam reared up onto her hind legs and thrust her front legs and head toward Callie's flower.

"Whoa!" Cressida yelled as she reached

again for the yellow sapphire. This time, she closed her hand around the cold, hard gemstone, and yelled out, "Got it!"

"Phew!" all six dunes yelled as they flattened to the ground, breathing hard and groaning. The flame-bite, shrieking and flailing, raced away.

"That was the hardest work I've ever done!" Darryl panted.

"You're telling me!" Denise said, trying to catch her breath.

Cressida scooted down Sunbeam's neck and onto her back before she slid to the ground. The yellow sapphire felt smooth and heavy in Cressida's hand, and she opened her fingers to see it up close. It shimmered in her palm.

"Good job, everyone!" Cressida said. "That was really hard, and you did it." Then she looked over at Sunbeam. "Are you ready to get your sapphire back?"

Sunbeam smiled with excitement and nodded. She bent her neck toward Cressida, and Cressida carefully placed the yellow sapphire in the empty circle in Sunbeam's blue necklace. Suddenly, Sunbeam's horn began to shimmer, and a brilliant ray of light came out from the tip. Sunbeam whinnied with joy.

The sun, bright and yellow, appeared in the sky. Soon, it was so warm that Cressida peeled off her yellow jacket and rolled up her sleeves. She fanned herself as she beheld the beauty of the Glitter Canyon. The sand glittered. The cacti, their prickles shining and their flowers opening, unfolded their arms and raised them toward the sky. The shimmering dunes slid and danced. A brilliant blue sky replaced the dim, gray one.

"Thank you, Cressida," Sunbeam said. "You've done an amazing job. You worked hard, and that hard work has paid off."

"I was happy to help," Cressida said. And she meant it.

"Let's go back to the palace!" Sunbeam said. "I can't wait to tell my sisters what you did!" She kneeled down, and Cressida climbed onto her back.

Chapter Nine

Back at the palace, the unicorn princesses crowded around Cressida. "Wow!" Flash said after Sunbeam told her sisters how Cressida had recovered the yellow sapphire from Callie's flower. "I had no idea human girls were so creative and smart."

Cressida smiled proudly.

"Amazing," said Bloom.

"Incredible," Prism added, nodding, so the amethyst on her necklace glittered.

Breeze, Moon, and Firefly flicked their manes and tails in agreement, and Cressida admired how beautiful all their gemstones looked in the brightly lit palace.

Then Flash looked at Sunbeam and whispered, so loud Cressida could hear her, "Do you want to give it to her, or do you want me to?"

"I'll do it," Sunbeam whispered. Flash nodded, though she looked disappointed.

Sunbeam turned and trotted down a long hallway with marble floors and chandeliers. Soon, she reappeared with a pink velvet pouch in her mouth.

"We, the princess unicorns, have a special

gift just for you," Flash said. The other unicorns fell silent and smiled.

Sunbeam walked right up to Cressida and dropped the pink pouch into her hands. Cressida's heart fluttered with excitement. She immediately recognized the shape of the gift inside the pouch. Grinning, she pulled out the key with the glowing crystal handle.

"It's your very own key to the Rainbow Realm!" Sunbeam exclaimed.

"We'd very much like you to have it," said Flash. Bloom, Prism, and all the other unicorns nodded.

"You're welcome to visit anytime you want," Sunbeam said. "And when we want to signal for you to return, we'll make the handle turn bright pink. Do you remember where the key goes, in the big oak tree?"

"Yes, I remember," said Cressida, wondering how she could ever forget that. "Thank you!" It was the best present she could imagine. She already couldn't wait for her next visit to the Rainbow Realm.

Just then, her stomach rumbled, and she realized she was hungry for more than just roinkleberries. And even though she didn't think she would tell her parents or Corey about her adventure—she knew they wouldn't believe her—she missed them. As if Sunbeam could read her mind, the unicorn said, "I bet you're ready to go home."

Cressida nodded. "I've had such an

amazing time here," she said. "But I should get back to my family. They'll be expecting me for breakfast."

"Anytime you're ready to leave the Rainbow Realm, all you need to do is close your eyes, put both hands on the handle of the key and say 'Take me home!'" Flash explained. "Why don't you try it now? And we'll see you again soon."

Cressida nodded. She waved good-bye to Flash, Bloom, Prism, Breeze, Moon, and Firefly. As she hugged Sunbeam, she said, "I'm so glad I could help you." She put both hands on the key's handle and closed her eyes. "Take me home!" she said. And then she added, "Please!"

Right away, Cressida felt a spinning

sensation. She opened her eyes. For an instant, she saw a blur of purple, silver, and white before everything went pitch black. This time, instead of a falling sensation, Cressida felt as though she were soaring upward. And then the flying sensation stopped, and the spinning slowed until she could see she was in the woods outside her house, lying on the ground next to the giant oak tree. For a moment, Cressida stared at the morning sky, with the puffy white clouds and the crows cawing from the tree branches. Finally, she sat up. She looked down at her key—her very own key to the Rainbow Realm—with its blue crystal handle, and slid it into her pocket. As she stood up, she noticed her yellow boots were gone, and she was yet again wearing her silver unicorn sneakers with the pink lights.

Cressida took a deep breath. She smiled. And then she ran home for breakfast with her parents and Corey, her unicorn sneakers blinking all the way.

Unicorn Princesses

Princesses

FLASH'S DASH

Chapter One

In the top tower of Spiral Palace, Ernest, a green wizard-lizard, placed two avocados on a chair. He smoothed his cape and straightened his pointy purple hat. With one scaly hand, he opened a thick, dusty book entitled *Intermediate Spells for Enterprising Wizard-Lizards*. With the other hand, he clutched a silver wand.

He cleared his throat. And then, reading from the book as he waved his wand at the avocados, he chanted, "Stickety Snickety Battery Goo! Pinkity Spinkity Strawberry Spew! Sleetily Sweetily Thickily Slew!" He waited. Nothing happened to the avocados. They didn't even quiver or jump.

"Huh," Ernest said. He repeated the spell. Again, nothing happened.

He wrinkled his brow and scratched his head. Then he checked his book. "Oh dear! Oh dear!" he muttered. "I read the wrong spell. Again. Oh dear! I thought that one sounded awfully strange."

Ernest rushed over to the window. Usually, when he cast the wrong spell, the sky darkened, thunder boomed, and lightning flashed. But this time the sun still shone in the cloudless blue sky above the Rainbow Realm. Just as he was about to breathe a sigh of relief, Ernest saw two bright pink clouds hovering over the Thunder Peaks. The clouds glittered and sparkled above the gold and silver mountains. And then, in a burst of light, the clouds vanished.

"Oh dear! I've done it again," Ernest muttered. "I guess I'll have to tell Flash." He sighed, scratched his head, and looked back at the avocados. He leafed through his book to find the spell he had meant to read, "Instructions for Turning Avocados into Flying Sneakers." And then, waving his wand, he chanted, "Fleetily Speedily

Fastily Foo! Wing Feet, Fleet Feet, Fast Feet, Blue!"

The two avocados trembled and spun in circles. They turned from purple to red to blue. And then, with a flash of gold so bright Ernest had to shield his eyes, two blue running shoes, each with a set of gold wings, appeared on the floor. Ernest

jumped with excitement and slid his scaly feet into the shoes.

"I did it! I did it!" he called out as he sprinted back and forth across the room. "Thunder Dash, here I come!"

Chapter Two

When Cressida Jenkins woke early on a Saturday morning, the unicorn lamp on her bed-side table still glowed, and her book, *Valley of the Unicorns*, lay face down on her pillow. She had, once again, fallen asleep reading. Cressida glanced at her new rainbow clock. It was 6:56 a.m. She sat up. She yawned and stretched. And then she opened her bedside table drawer and pulled out the key the unicorn princesses had given to her. It was a large, old-fashioned silver key with a crystal ball handle that changed colors.

That morning, the key's handle glowed orange, like a jack-o'-lantern. Cressida wrapped her hands around the key and remembered how she'd gotten it. On a walk in the woods with her family, she had found the key under a giant oak tree and slipped it into her pocket. The next morning, worried someone—perhaps even a magical forest creature, like a fairy or a troll—might look for it, she returned to the woods to leave the key where she found it. That's when she met the key's owner, a yellow unicorn named Princess Sunbeam.

It turned out Sunbeam was searching for a human girl who believed in unicorns to help her find her magic gemstone—a yellow sapphire that had disappeared when Ernest the wizard-lizard accidentally cast the wrong spell.

Cressida accompanied Sunbeam to the Rainbow Realm, an enchanted world ruled by seven unicorn princesses who each wore a unique gemstone necklace that gave them magic powers. After Cressida found Sunbeam's yellow sapphire, the princesses gave Cressida her very own key to the Rainbow Realm. "You're welcome to visit anytime you want," Sunbeam had said. "And when we want to signal for you to return, we'll make the handle turn bright pink." Now

Cressida smiled, remembering that magic day with Sunbeam.

Since it was Saturday, and since she had already finished all her math and reading homework, Cressida decided to visit the Rainbow Realm that day. She missed her unicorn friends. But first she wanted to eat breakfast and read another chapter of her book. She only had four chapters left, and when she finished it she would have read every book about unicorns in her elementary school's library.

Cressida returned the key to her bedside table drawer and climbed out of bed. She peeled off her green unicorn pajamas, and put on rainbow leggings and a blue sweater with a purple sequined unicorn on the front. She tiptoed into the kitchen. Her older brother, Corey, and her parents were still asleep, and she didn't want to wake them. She poured herself a bowl of Whole Wheat Squares and ate her cereal quickly: she couldn't wait to get back to her book.

When she finished, Cressida put her empty bowl in the sink and crept back to her bedroom, climbed onto the bed, and found her place in *Valley of the Unicorns*. But after she had only read a few sentences, she heard a soft, high noise. It sounded, Cressida thought, like wind chimes or someone playing a triangle.

Cressida looked up. The noise went away. She waited several seconds, shrugged, and returned to her book. But just as she was about to turn to the next page, the chiming returned. Cressida listened for a moment. It sounded like it was coming from her bedside table drawer. She put down her book, opened the drawer, and pulled out the key again. The handle glowed bright pink and pulsed. She held the key up to her ear, and, sure enough, it was making the tinkling noise. Cressida grinned with excitement. The unicorn princesses were inviting her back to the Rainbow Realm!

Cressida bounded to her closet and slid her feet into her silver unicorn sneakers, which had bright pink lights that blinked every time she walked, ran, or jumped. She raced into the kitchen and left a note on the table for her parents saying she'd gone

for a quick walk. Luckily, when Cressida entered the Rainbow Realm, time in the human world froze. That meant she could stay with the unicorns as long as she wanted without her parents worrying about her or wondering where she was.

Gripping the key in her right hand, Cressida sprinted out her back door, bounded into the woods, and ran along the path that led to the oak tree. The pink lights on her sneakers blinked the whole way, and Cressida couldn't remember ever feeling so excited. Once she got to the oak tree, she kneeled down to the base of the trunk, near the roots. "Here I come!" Cressida whispered, and she pushed the key into the tiny keyhole Sunbeam had shown her.

With a jolt, the forest and sky began to spin, faster and faster, until all Cressida could see was a blur of brown, green, and blue. Then everything went pitch black, and she felt as though she were falling fast through space.

Suddenly, she landed on something soft and velvety. For a moment, she felt dizzy, and all she could see was a revolving blur of white, purple, pink, and silver. Soon, as Cressida blinked and took deep breaths, the room stopped spinning, and she knew exactly where she was: sitting on a plush purple armchair in Spiral Palace, the unicorn princesses' white, shimmering castle that was shaped like a giant unicorn horn.

Chapter Three

C ressida inhaled. The palace smelled like lavender, mint, and honey. Sunlight poured in through the floor-to-ceiling windows, and the purple velvet curtains swayed in the breeze. Cressida stood up. "Hello?" she called out. "It's me, Cressida!" She listened for the tapping of hooves against the marble floors, but all she heard was the faint sound of harp music playing in another room.

Cressida wondered if she should look for the unicorns, but as she walked toward a hallway, she heard hooves pounding the ground outside. The noise was so thunderous she wondered if an entire herd of unicorns was stampeding toward the palace. She ran to the window. Looking outside, Cressida saw all seven unicorn princesses racing up the hill toward Spiral Palace, their heads down and their horns pointed straight ahead.

In the lead galloped silver Princess Flash. Behind her sprinted purple Princess Prism. Next trotted blue Princess Breeze, orange Princess Firefly, and black Princess Moon.

Behind all the other unicorns, breathing hard as they trudged uphill, were yellow Princess Sunbeam and green Princess Bloom.

Flash, Prism, Breeze, Firefly, and Moon clattered in through the palace's front door and headed straight for a silver trough of water. They drank quickly and rushed over to Cressida.

"Cressida!" they exclaimed, rearing up on their hind legs. "We were hoping you would come!" Just then, Sunbeam and Bloom dragged themselves into the palace, pink-cheeked and panting. They both nearly fell into the trough, where they guzzled water as though they hadn't had a drink in weeks.

After several seconds, Sunbeam raised her head and grinned at Cressida. "I'm so glad you're here!" Sunbeam said, water dripping from her chin as she tried to catch her breath. "I've missed you so much!" She lowered her head back into the trough for several more gulps before she danced over to Cressida and kneeled down. "Climb up!" she cried. "I'm exhausted from our run, but not too tired to dance around the palace with you on my back!"

Cressida swung her leg over Sunbeam's back, grabbed Sunbeam's silky yellow mane in her hands, and laughed as the unicorn pranced across the room, singing, "My human girl is back! My human girl is back!"

Sunbeam inhaled loudly. "You know, you still don't smell!"

Cressida giggled. Last time she had visited, Sunbeam confessed she had always believed human girls smelled bad. "You don't smell bad, either," Cressida replied.

"That's good, since I've been running all morning," Sunbeam said. Then she blushed and looked down at her hooves. "Well, honestly, I also did a lot of walking. And I took some breaks to sit down and rest. But even still, I'm really, really tired. I hate to say it, but I'm so tired that I think you'd better get off my back."

"No problem," Cressida said, and she slid off Sunbeam.

Flash, who had been stretching on the

other side of the room, joined Cressida and Sunbeam. "You did a great job this morning," Flash said to Sunbeam. "The only way to get better at running is to keep doing it, even when it's hard. That's what I did."

Sunbeam rolled her eyes. "Flash thinks she's better than the rest of us because she goes for a long run every morning," she whispered to Cressida.

"I heard that!" Flash said, but her face broke into a smile. "And I don't think I'm better than all my sisters. I just love to run."

Cressida nodded. She loved to run, too.

"Anyway," Flash said, the magic diamond on her necklace glittering in the light of the chandelier, "I bet you're wondering why we invited you back to the Rainbow Realm."

"Well," Cressida said, "the question had crossed my mind." She couldn't wait to hear what the unicorn princesses were up to.

"So," Flash and Sunbeam said at the same time. They looked at each other. "Well," they both began again.

"I'll tell her," Sunbeam said, sounding annoyed.

"No, I will," Flash said, her voice firm.

"I'm the one that found her," Sunbeam said. "She was my friend first."

Flash sniffed. "The Thunder Dash takes place in my domain. Last time she visited, you got to spend the whole time with her. Now it's my turn."

"But she likes me more," Sunbeam protested.

"No, she likes me more," Flash insisted, flicking her tail and mane.

"Hold on!" Cressida said. "Please stop arguing!"

Sunbeam and Flash, both scowling, looked away from each other.

"Take a deep breath," Cressida said. The unicorns wrinkled their noses. But then they both inhaled slowly and exhaled. "Listen," Cressida said, "I like both of you the same amount, which is a whole, whole lot. I'm sure I'll be able to spend time with both of you during this visit."

Sunbeam and Flash looked calmer, but Cressida could see in their eyes they both still felt a little angry. "Let's take one more deep breath," Cressida said, "the three of us together. And then you can tell me all about the Thunder Dash."

Cressida, Sunbeam, and Flash all sucked in their breath and then exhaled so loudly and forcefully that Flash accidentally snorted. The three of them burst out giggling, and Cressida was relieved to see the sisters looked like they had forgiven each other.

"You can tell Cressida about the Thunder Dash," Sunbeam said. "You're right that it takes place in your domain."

Flash grinned excitedly and swished her

tail. Her eyes glittered. "The reason we invited you here," she began, "is we're going to hold the Thunder Dash this afternoon. I host it every year in my realm, the Thunder Peaks."

"Thanks so much for the invitation," Cressida said. "What, exactly, is the Thunder Dash?"

"It's a running race," explained Flash. "And this year, it will be different than ever before. In the past, only unicorns have competed, and all the other creatures in the Rainbow Realm cheered us on. But this year, we've opened the race to everyone. We were wondering if you want to be the first human girl to run in the Thunder Dash."

Cressida's heart swelled with excitement. She couldn't think of anything that sounded more fun. "I can't wait," Cressida said. She jumped up and down, so her silver unicorn sneakers blinked.

Just then, a lizard wearing a purple cloak and a tall, pointy hat rushed into the room, running upright on his two back feet. He wore blue sneakers with flapping gold wings that lifted him into the air with each step. "Cressida Jenkins? Is it you? The human girl who believes in unicorns?" he asked in a high, nasal voice. Cressida smiled at the funny green creature. "I'm Ernest the wizard-lizard." He held out a hand for Cressida to shake.

"It's a pleasure to meet you," Cressida said, kneeling and trying not to giggle as his cold scales and claws tickled her palm.

"I have a present for you," said Ernest, grinning proudly. And then he reached into the pocket of his cloak and pulled out a pair of gold running shorts and a gold T-shirt with a picture of two silver wings on the front. "I made these for you out of two bananas. It took me a few tries because I kept making teal dirt and cold warts instead of a T-shirt and gold shorts. Can you believe it? But I finally got it right."

Flash, Sunbeam, and all the other unicorn princesses rolled their eyes and smiled at Ernest as Cressida admired her new running outfit. "Thank you so much," Cressida said. She looked at Flash. "Is there somewhere I could change my clothes?"

"No need for that!" called out Ernest. And then he waved his wand at Cressida and chanted, "Changety Switchety Windily Woo! Goldily Clothety Runnily Roo!" Cressida felt wind swirling around her body, as though she stood at the center of a miniature tornado. When the wind stopped, the gold shorts were inside out and upside down on her chest, and the gold shirt hung from her waist like a skirt.

"Oh dear! Oh dear!" said Ernest. "Hold on a minute! Let me try again!" He waved the wand and repeated the spell. Cressida felt another swirl of wind. Then she smiled

with relief. This time the shirt was on top, and the shorts were right side out.

"Thank you, Ernest," Cressida said. "I can't wait to wear my new shorts and T-shirt for the Thunder Dash!"

"No problem!" Ernest said, beaming proudly. Then he looked at Flash. "Um," he said, fidgeting and looking down at his sneakers. "When I was making my new running shoes, there was a bit of a very, very small mishap when I, *ahem*, read the wrong spell. Twice. I'm sure it's nothing. Nothing at all. But, *um*, if you notice anything a little strange in the Thunder Peaks, that's why."

Flash opened her mouth to respond, but before she could say anything, Ernest pulled a watch on a long gold chain from his pocket and cried, "Oh dear! Look at the time! I'd better go! I need to get in one last training run before the Thunder Dash this afternoon." And then he sprinted from the room.

"That Ernest," Flash said, shaking her

head. "He's always up to something. I'm sure I'll find flying lemons or jumping mangos waiting for me when I get back to the Thunder Peaks."

The other unicorn princesses laughed and nodded.

Cressida smiled at the thought of Ernest's magical mishaps. And she was glad she had finally gotten to meet the wizard-lizard she had heard so much about. "It sure was nice of Ernest to make me these new running clothes," she said, twirling around. "How do I look?"

"Fast!" said Flash. "Like a bolt of lightning! You'll be a streak of gold when you run this afternoon."

Sunbeam smiled and nodded, but

Cressida could see in Sunbeam's eyes that the unicorn felt worried and anxious.

Flash noticed, too. "What's wrong?" she asked her youngest sister.

Sunbeam shrugged. "I just don't really want to run in the Thunder Dash this year. I'm sick of always coming in last. It's embarrassing."

"Oh Sunbeam," Flash said. "I've told you a hundred times. If you practiced running more, you'd be faster, and then you'd enjoy the Thunder Dash."

Sunbeam snorted. "You've definitely told me that more than a hundred times. Besides, the only reason you always win is because you cheat. You use your magic to run faster than everyone else."

Hurt and surprise filled Flash's eyes. "I would never cheat. I'm fast because I run every morning, every day of the year. Whenever I invite you to join me, you stop to sunbathe and eat roinkleberries."

"I do not," snapped Sunbeam. "You're a cheater."

"I most certainly am not," Flash said, stomping her hoof.

The other unicorns stared at Flash and Sunbeam. "There they go again," whispered Prism to Breeze. Moon and Firefly nodded. Bloom, who seemed to side with Sunbeam, swished her tail and glared at Flash.

"Please stop shouting," Cressida said. "We all lose our tempers sometimes.

Especially when we feel hurt." She smiled sympathetically at Sunbeam. "It sounds like Flash is proud of how hard she's worked to be a fast runner, and she feels hurt when you accuse her of cheating." And then Cressida looked at Flash. "It sounds like Sunbeam might not like running as much as you do. And that's okay. We can't all be good at everything."

Flash took a long deep breath. Sunbeam sighed. And then they both nodded.

"I'm sorry, Flash," Sunbeam said. She yawned, and her eyelids began to droop. "I'm really tired, and that makes me cranky. I think I'd better take a nap." Cressida noticed Bloom had already fallen fast asleep on a pink velvet couch. Now Sunbeam climbed up next to her sister.

"Apology accepted," said Flash. "Will you and Bloom meet me in the Thunder Peaks after you wake up?"

"Yes," Sunbeam said as her heavy eyelids drooped shut. Soon, both Bloom and Sunbeam were snoring. Cressida smiled at the sight of the yellow and green unicorns curled up together. She hoped Sunbeam would feel better after she slept.

Flash, full of energy, flicked her mane and shuffled her silver hooves. "I'm about to gallop back to the Thunder Peaks to finish preparing for the Dash," she said to Cressida. Want to join me?"

"Of course!" said Cressida.

Flash reared up and whinnied. "I can't wait to show you the Thunder Peaks! Climb up!" she said. "And get ready for a fast ride!"

Chapter Four

C ressida sat on Flash's back and gripped the unicorn's shimmering silver mane. While Sunbeam's mane reminded Cressida of thin threads of yellow silk, Flash's mane seemed more like glittery strands of Christmas tree tinsel. Flash trotted out the palace's front door, and, as soon as her hooves hit the clear stones that led away from Spiral Palace, she began to gallop. As Flash picked up speed, the wind riffled through Cressida's dark hair. Cressida guessed they were going faster than when she glided down a steep hill on her bike or rode a roller coaster at the state fair.

"Want to go even faster?" asked Flash, sounding playful and daring.

Cressida's eyes widened. How could Flash run any faster? "Is that possible?" she called out, laughing.

"As you know, my magic power is to run so fast that my horn and hooves create lightning," Flash explained. "Despite what Sunbeam said, I never use my magic powers when I'm training for the Thunder Dash or in the race itself. But I don't see any harm in using it now, just for fun. What do you think?"

"I'm ready!" Cressida said, tightening her grip on Flash's mane.

And then, suddenly, Flash surged forward, running so fast Cressida wondered if they were flying. Cressida squealed with delight as silver and gold lightning bolts crackled from Flash's horn and hooves.

Now, Cressida was quite sure they were sprinting as fast as a cheetah. "Wheeeeee!" Cressida yelled as Flash sped along a thin, winding forest path. Squirrels and chipmunks stopped chasing each other and searching for nuts to stare at Flash and Cressida. Woodland fairies, with silver wings, called out, "Whoa!" and "Look at them go!" as they peered out from behind giant toadstools. Three baby skunks sprinted alongside Flash and Cressida, trying to keep up, but they soon fell behind and collapsed on the forest floor, breathless and giggling.

Soon, Flash and Cressida came to a long, straight stretch of the forest trail. "Are you ready?" Flash sang out.

Before Cressida could ask, "For what?" Flash leaped into the air, soaring for several seconds before she landed and jumped again.

"We're flying!" Cressida called out as even more lightning sizzled and sparked from Flash's horn and hooves.

Just as Cressida began to feel dizzy and a little sick to her stomach, the trail narrowed and began to turn sharply. Flash slowed down, first to a slow gallop, then a trot, and then a fast walk.

"Phew!" Flash exclaimed, breathless. "That was the most fun I've had in weeks!"

"Me too!" said Cressida.

"I love magic sprinting and leaping even more when you're riding me," said Flash.

"And guess what? We're almost to the Thunder Peaks. So close your eyes!" Cressida shut her eyes and smiled, excited to see Flash's domain. After a few seconds, Flash said, "We're here!"

Cressida opened her eyes to behold a meadow with silvery green, gold, copper, and bronze grass, dotted with blue and purple wildflowers. Copper-colored rabbits, with long ears, hopped through the flowers and chewed on leaves. Golden-orange fox cubs chased each other and tumbled through the grass. Red and bronze butterflies swooped and fluttered. Just behind the meadow towered two of the highest mountains Cressida had ever seen. Minty green pine trees, ferns, and round metallic boulders covered both mountains. In the sunlight, the boulders glittered so brightly Cressida squinted as her eyes adjusted to the light.

"Well? What do you think?" Flash asked, kneeling down so Cressida could slide off her back. Cressida stepped into a patch of silvery green grass, and stared at the meadow and the mountains. They were so stunning Cressida had trouble finding the right words. "Amazing," she finally said. Three baby rabbits jumped over to Cressida and began to nibble the grass. Cressida kneeled down and held out her hand to them. She expected the rabbits to run away, but instead they hopped closer to her. Cressida scooped one up in her

arms, and he nuzzled against her chest and closed his eyes.

Flash glanced at the baby rabbit and smiled. Then she pointed her horn toward one of the Thunder Peaks. "See that path that goes straight up the mountain?" Flash asked. Cressida looked out into the distance as she stroked the baby rabbit's head. She saw a long, bright pink line that started at the base of the mountain and ended at the gold-capped top. "That's the racecourse we use for the Thunder Dash."

"What makes it so pink?" asked Cressida. It was even pinker, Cressida decided, than her favorite pink unicorn raincoat.

"Pink? It's not pi—" Flash began. But her voice trailed off when she lifted her head to look more closely at the mountain. "That's really odd," Flash said slowly. "The path is paved with crushed diamonds. It usually looks white and glittery."

"Should we go check it out?" asked Cressida. Just then, the baby rabbit nudged Cressida's arm and nodded toward the ground. Cressida petted his soft head one more time and placed him back in the patch of grass with his brother and sister.

As Flash and Cressida walked across the meadow toward the pink racecourse, the rabbits nodded at Cressida and the foxes waved. Cressida smiled and waved back. A butterfly landed on her nose, and she giggled until it fluttered away. As

Cressida got closer to the animals, she noticed something funny: many were wearing bright green sneakers.

"Where did all the animals get their running shoes?" Cressida asked.

Flash grinned. "I gave all the creatures in the Thunder Peaks sneakers as a gift. They're very excited to be running in the Thunder Dash for the first time this year."

"I bet," Cressida said.

On the other side of the meadow, at the base of the mountain, Flash and Cressida wove through a thicket of pine trees and then, suddenly, stopped short. "Look at that!" Flash gasped, her eyes wide. There, in front of them, was the start of the path the unicorns used for the Thunder Dash, and it was covered in thick, bright pink mud.

Flash lifted a silver hoof, and touched the pink muck. Immediately, her leg sunk down. "Whoa!" Flash said, laughing. She put another leg into the mud. Then she lifted one of her hooves and stomped down, so pink mud splattered everywhere. Cressida giggled as tiny drops landed on her face, arms, and legs.

"Come on in!" Flash called out, leaping forward so all four hooves sunk into the mud with a giant splash. "I think this is Ernest's best magical mishap yet!"

Cressida giggled and stepped cautiously toward the mud. She wanted to play with Flash, but she also didn't want to ruin her unicorn sneakers. Just then, her eye caught something glittery at the base of a pine tree. She turned and saw two shimmering silver rain boots with a note on them that read, Dear Cressida, It was wonderful to meet you today. Sincerely, Ernest. Cressida hurriedly took off her sneakers and slipped on the boots. They fit perfectly.

Flash looked at Cressida's boots and said, "Those are even shinier than my horn and hooves!"

Cressida grinned, marched over to the pink mud, and stepped in. The mud came halfway up her boots, and it felt thicker and stickier than she expected.

"Maybe even Sunbeam and Bloom will like running in this!" Flash said as she stomped. "We could call this year's race the Thunder-Mud Dash!"

"Or the Thunder *Splash*!" Cressida suggested, twirling and stomping as hard as she could, to splatter the pink mud. Soon, they were both stomping in circles, squealing with delight as pink mud rained down on them.

Then Flash, who had several large globs of pink mud on her nose, paused. She sniffed several times. "Do you smell strawberries?"

Cressida inhaled. Her nose caught only the faintest whiff of strawberries. "I think so," she said slowly.

"I'm sure I do," Flash said. Then, with her silver tongue, she licked the pink mud from her nose. Her eyes widened and she smiled before she lapped up more mud. "Try it!" she said, and she stomped, sending a shower of pink mud right into Cressida's face.

Cressida giggled and wiped off her face with her hand. Then, feeling a little unsure, she licked some of the mud off her fingers. It tasted wonderful and sweet. She laughed. The mud wasn't mud at all. It was strawberry cake batter! And not only that, but it was the best strawberry cake batter she had ever had. "Yum!" Cressida said. She began to lick cake batter off her arms and hands while Flash bowed down and ate some right off the racecourse.

After several minutes of licking the

batter, Flash said, "If I eat any more of this, I'll be too full to run in the Dash!"

"Me too," agreed Cressida.

"Plus," Flash said, "as much fun as we're having, we better get ready for the race. It won't be long before my sisters and all the creatures in the Rainbow Realm arrive ready to run. We need to put up the starting line and the finish line. And we're in a bit of a rush."

"How can I help?" asked Cressida.

"Do you think you could walk up to the top of the mountain and hang the finish line?" Flash asked.

"Definitely!" Cressida said, looking excitedly at the long, pink path leading to the mountain's peak. She couldn't wait to climb up it!

"Great! Thanks, Cressida," Flash said. "I'll stay down here in case anyone gets here early. I'm sure the foxes will be happy to help me hang the starting line and the race flags."

Chapter Five

A fox wearing green sneakers and a yellow visor appeared from behind a boulder carrying a clipboard, two rolled-up ribbons, and a stack of triangular flags.

"Thank you, Frederick," Flash said. "Why don't you give the finish line to my friend, Cressida? She's going to climb up the mountain and hang it for us. And after that, she's going to be the first human girl to run in the Thunder Dash!"

"Well, congratulations!" Frederick said, smiling. "And thanks for your help preparing for the Dash." He handed Cressida one of the ribbons.

"Thank you. I'll be back soon!" she said. She put the finish line in her pocket and began hiking uphill, through the cake batter.

As Cressida walked, the batter got deeper and deeper. Soon, it reached the very tops of her boots. She knew the unicorns would be able to gallop right through it, but she worried the smaller creatures in the Rainbow Realm might struggle to even walk, let alone run, in it. Just then,

Cressida's foot got stuck in an especially thick, deep spot. She tugged and yanked at her boot until it finally came out with a splash.

"Phew!" Cressida said as batter splattered her face.

She decided to take a break from wading through the batter and to instead climb the mountain by scaling the gigantic boulders that covered the Thunder peaks.

She waded over to a gold boulder next to the racecourse, grabbed the top and pulled herself up. As Cressida slid across it, she heard a yawn. And then, for a second, the boulder seemed to jump ever so slightly. Cressida paused, and the boulder stopped moving. She shrugged, leaped to the ground, ran across a log coated in coppery green moss, and began scaling a silver boulder. As soon as she had scrambled to the top, the boulder began to hop.

"Yikes!" said Cressida, almost sliding off.

"Well, hello there!" the boulder called out. "I bet you didn't think you'd be riding a boulder this morning, now did you?"

Cressida laughed. "Hello," she said. After talking to sand dunes and cacti during her last visit to the Rainbow Realm, Cressida wasn't surprised to be conversing with a boulder.

"I'm Boris!" the boulder bellowed, jumping even higher. "Boris the bouncing boulder! And that's Beatrice that you just

climbed over. She's less bouncy than I am today because she went to the Boulder Smolder last night."

"The Boulder Smolder?" Cressida asked. "What's that?"

"Well," said Boris, spinning as he jumped, "we boulders are nocturnal. That means we sleep all day, and we're awake all night."

"Like raccoons and bats," Cressida said. She had learned about nocturnal animals in her science class.

"Precisely!" exclaimed Boris. "Well, every night we boulders hold a Boulder Smolder, where we build a huge bonfire and jump in and out of it! All night long! That makes us good and tired so we can sleep all day."

"Don't you get burned?" Cressida asked.

"Oh no!" laughed Boris. "We boulders love fire. It's never too hot for us. I was planning on going to the Boulder Smolder last night, but I decided to stay home and play with my new marbles. Today I have so much energy I can hardly hold still, let alone sleep."

"I see that," Cressida said, tightening her grip on Boris. She felt as though she were on a trampoline.

"So," Boris said, "who are you, and what brings you to the Thunder Peaks?"

"I'm Cressida Jenkins. I'm friends with Flash."

"Pleasure to meet you!" Boris said.

Just then, Cressida heard two voices calling out from farther up the mountain. "Help!" the voices yelled. "We're stuck! Please help us!"

"Who is that?" Cressida asked, concerned.

"Felicity and Felix," Boris said. "They've

been shouting all morning. I'll take you to them." With that, Boris began to bounce up the mountain.

Every few bounces, he collided with other boulders who yawned and mumbled, "Watch it," and, "I'm trying to sleep."

Finally, Boris landed next to the racecourse, near the mountain's peak. In the middle of the path, poking out of the pink batter, were the heads and tails of two golden-orange foxes.

"My name is Cressida Jenkins," Cressida said, sliding off Boris and rushing over to the edge of the racecourse. "I heard you calling for help."

"Thank goodness!" one of the foxes said. She smiled and her copper eyes twinkled. "My name is Felicity. This is my brother, Felix."

"It's a delight to meet you, even under these strange circumstances," Felix said, twitching his gold whiskers. "We were running this morning when two pink clouds appeared. Then, the next thing we knew, strawberry cake batter rained down on us, and then we got stuck. It was the strangest thing I've ever seen!"

"At least we haven't been hungry while we've been waiting for help," Felicity added as she lapped some batter from her nose.

"I'll certainly try my best to get you out," Cressida said. She reached her arms toward Felicity. "Do you think you can pull out your two front paws and put them in my hands?"

The fox struggled for a few seconds, and then, with a grunt, placed her two front feet in Cressida's palms. Cressida closed her hands tightly around Felicity's green sneakers, both dripping in cake batter.

"One. Two. Three," Cressida counted out loud, and then she pulled as hard as she could. She could feel Felicity straining to lift her hind feet or jump. But the batter was too sticky and thick. Felicity was still stuck.

"Oh no," Felix said, biting his bottom lip. "We'll be here forever."

A tear slid down Felicity's cheek.

"Don't panic yet," Cressida said, trying

to sound reassuring. "I have one more idea." She turned to Boris. "If I lie across you and hold on to Felicity's paws, will you bounce as high as you can?"

"Sure thing!" Boris said.

Cressida climbed onto Boris and again reached out to Felicity. The fox sniffled, took a deep breath, and put her paws back in Cressida's hands.

"Okay, Boris," called out Cressida, "Bounce!"

"That's what I do best!" Boris bellowed as he jumped as high as he could, easily yanking Felicity out of the cake batter.

"Please try to land carefully!" Cressida said, holding tightly to Felicity as the boulder soared toward the sky and then hurtled downward.

To Cressida's surprise, Boris landed gently on a bed of pine needles.

"Phew!" said Felicity, sliding off Boris and twirling around in a circle. "Thank you!" She began to lick cake batter off her arms, legs, stomach, and back.

"I'm glad to help," Cressida said. Then she looked at Boris. "Let's get Felix out."

Cressida climbed onto Boris and grabbed Felix's front feet, which he had managed to yank from the batter. Boris rolled back and launched himself high in the air, pulling Felix with him.

"I'm afraid of heights!" Felix said, sounding panicked as they flew upward.

"I won't let you fall!" Cressida said, squeezing Felix's green sneakers.

Boris landed again in the pine needles. Felix jumped off Boris and ran to hug Felicity. "We're free!" he called out. "Thank you!"

"I'm so glad I could help, and it's been wonderful to meet you," Cressida said. "I hate to hurry off, but I better get up to the top to hang the finish line for Flash. And then I need to tell her we need to get all this cake batter off the racecourse before the Thunder Dash. It's too deep, thick, and sticky for anyone but a unicorn to run through!"

"We'd be glad to hang the finish line while you go talk to Flash," Felicity offered.

Felix nodded. "We know exactly where it goes."

"Thanks!" Cressida said, and she pulled the finish line from her pocket and handed it to Felicity. The two foxes began making their way up the mountain, darting around boulders and climbing logs to get to the top.

"I'll take you to Flash in no time," said Boris, hopping over to Cressida. "Jump aboard!"

Chapter Six

Cressida climbed onto Boris. He bounced down the mountain, crashing into other boulders who yawned and mumbled, "You should have gone to the Boulder Smolder, Boris. You have way too much energy today."

At the bottom of the mountain, Cressida slid off Boris to find Flash at the base of the racecourse giving a team of foxes instructions about where to hang flags and place large troughs of water. "Is the finish line up?" Flash asked.

"Well," said Cressida, "we have a bit of a complication." She told Flash about how thick and deep the cake batter got farther up the racecourse, and about saving Felicity and Felix.

Flash's mouth bent into a worried frown. "Oh no," she said. "The Thunder Dash is supposed to start in less than an hour. How can we possibly clear the course that quickly? I'm worried we'll have to cancel the race." To Cressida's surprise, tears welled up in Flash's eyes.

Cressida put her arms around the

unicorn's silver neck and squeezed. "It's true that we might have to cancel the race," Cressida said. "But before we do, let's see if we can think of a way to quickly clear the course."

Just then, a voice called out from across the meadow: "What's wrong? Did you pull a muscle running?" Cressida and Flash turned to see Sunbeam galloping toward them with Bloom behind her. On Bloom's back rode Ernest, wearing his blue, winged sneakers. Cressida was glad to see that Sunbeam and Bloom now looked much more energetic.

"Look!" said Flash, pointing her horn toward the path. "There's strawberry cake batter all over the racecourse. If we can't think of a way to clean it up, we'll have to cancel the Thunder Dash."

Ernest's bottom jaw dropped. His eyes widened. He slapped both his scaly palms against his forehead. "Oh dear! Oh no!" he called out. "I was thinking there would be just a puddle, or maybe two!"

Flash looked forlornly at the cake batter. "Is there any way to undo the spell?" she asked.

"Well, um, no," said Ernest. "I already looked it up. I'm so sorry, Flash!"

Cressida's heart sank. While she didn't feel as disappointed as Flash, she had been awfully excited to be the first human girl to run in the Dash. "There has to be a way to clean up this cake batter," she said, sucking in her bottom lip exactly the way she did when she was solving a math homework problem.

"I doubt it," said Sunbeam. Cressida turned and saw that Sunbeam did not look even a little disappointed about canceling the Thunder Dash. In fact, Sunbeam's eyes glittered with excitement.

"I can't think of a way to clean it up, either," Bloom added, shrugging. She, too, seemed perfectly happy to skip the race.

"What if we asked all the foxes and rabbits to eat the cake batter?" Cressida suggested.

"That's a good idea, but I think there's just way too much of it," Flash said. "Plus, if they eat cake batter now, they'll feel too sick to run."

Cressida nodded.

"Oh well," said Sunbeam, "I guess we'll just have to cancel the race. Sorry, Flash."

Sunbeam looked like she might start doing a celebratory dance. "Why don't you come join me in my domain, the Glitter Canyon, instead? We can sunbathe in the purple sand. There's even a new patch of violets we can roll around in."

Cressida wasn't in the mood to sunbathe or roll around in violets. She felt like running and racing. "Sunbeam," Cressida said slowly as she stared at the pink batter. "I know your magic power is to control the sun. But you can also make heat come from your horn, right?"

"Sure," said Sunbeam, and she pointed her horn toward the sky. Yellow, sparkling light streamed out, and immediately Cressida felt a gust of hot air.

"And Bloom," Cressida said. "You can make objects grow and shrink, right?"

"Yep," said Bloom, and she pointed her horn toward a copper-colored pinecone on the ground. A beam of emerald light shot from her horn, and the pinecone shrank to the size of a sesame seed. "But I don't know what good that does us now," Bloom said. "Let's go sunbathe!"

"Wait!" exclaimed Cressida, jumping up and down. "I have an idea that will get all the strawberry cake batter off the race-course just in time for the Thunder Dash!"

Flash's eyes widened and sparkled. "What can I do to help?" she asked.

"Well," said Cressida, smiling encouragingly at Sunbeam and Bloom, "we'll mostly need to get help from Sunbeam, Bloom, and the boulders."

Sunbeam's face fell. "I think we should just go sunbathe," she said. "I don't really feel like using my magic right now. I'm still tired from my training run." Bloom nodded in agreement.

"Sunbeam," Cressida said gently, "can we talk for a minute over there?" Cressida pointed to a patch of blue wildflowers under a gnarled copper-and-green pine tree.

"Sure," Sunbeam said. Cressida and Sunbeam walked over to the wildflowers.

"Sunbeam," Cressida said, "it seems like you really don't want to run in the Thunder Dash."

"I'm just really sick of losing. And," she said, letting out a heavy sigh, "yesterday while I was on a training run, the boulders said I look funny when I trot. I used to like running in the Dash. It was fun to run with my sisters, even though I always came in last. But now, after hearing the boulders say that, I don't ever want to run again."

"I can completely understand that," said Cressida. "My older brother used to tease me about how I kicked the soccer ball. I wanted to quit the team, but my parents wouldn't let me. I kept playing, and now soccer is one of my favorite sports. I'm not the best player, but I really enjoy it."

Sunbeam looked thoughtful. "I guess you have a point," she finally said. "If the boulders hadn't said that, I'd still like running in the Dash. I know I shouldn't let them keep me from having a good time. But every time I think about it, I just want the race to be canceled forever."

"Well," said Cressida, "I think the Thunder Dash really means a lot to Flash. So, how about if we go talk to the boulders who teased you. If you feel better afterward, will you help remove the cake batter from the course so Flash doesn't have to cancel the race?"

"Talk to the boulders?" Sunbeam said, looking nervous.

"I'll come with you. And we could even ask Flash to come, too."

Sunbeam took a long, deep breath, as

though she were summoning all her courage. "Okay. I'll try talking to the boulders. And if they apologize and promise not to tease me again, I'll help clear the racecourse. But I don't want Flash to come. I want to prove to myself that I can do this without my big sister's help. Plus, I don't think I can stand to hear her tell me about the importance of practicing even one more time."

Cressida nodded. She often didn't like getting advice from her older brother, either. "Sounds like a good plan," she said. "Which boulders said you looked funny?"

"It was Boris. And his sister Beatrice," Sunbeam said.

"It just so happens I met them this

morning," Cressida said as she and Sunbeam walked together toward the boulders. They found Boris and Beatrice playing with a set of marbles next to a thick patch of ferns.

"Boris and Beatrice," said Cressida. "Sunbeam and I are wondering if we might talk to you for a moment." The two boulders looked up. Beatrice looked sleepy, with droopy gold eyelids, but Boris seemed wide awake.

"Sure!" bellowed Boris.

"Well—" began Cressida.

But Sunbeam interrupted her. "I wanted to say," said Sunbeam, "that I felt really hurt and angry when you said I looked funny when I was running here yesterday. I enjoyed running before I heard you say that. And now I feel too self-conscious to race in the Dash."

"Funny?" said Boris, looking confused. He turned to Beatrice. "Did we say Sunbeam looked *funny*?"

"I don't think so," said Beatrice, furrowing her gold brow. "No, not that I can recall. I remember you saying she looked sunny. Like a blur of yellow sunshine."

Recognition came over Boris's face. "That's right! We were watching Sunbeam run, and I called out to her that she looked downright sunny. You know, like a streak of yellow and light." Then he looked back at Sunbeam. "I think you heard us wrong. I never would have said you look funny, because you don't! Plus, that wouldn't be a very nice thing for a boulder, who can't even run, to say about a unicorn. And a unicorn princess at that."

Relief washed over Sunbeam's face. Then she smiled proudly. "Sunny when I run!" she repeated. "Well, thank you for the compliment!"

"You're most welcome," Boris and Beatrice said in unison.

"Sunbeam," Cressida said, "are you willing to help get the racecourse ready for the Thunder Dash?"

"I sure am," said Sunbeam. "Just tell me what you need me to do, and I'll do it!"

"Super," said Cressida. Then she looked at Boris and Beatrice. "I have a plan to get

rid of all that cake batter, but I need the help of all the boulders on the mountain. Do you think you and the other boulders could build an archway over the entire racecourse?"

"An archway?" Boris and Beatrice said at once. "What's that?"

"Well," Cressida said. She knew all about archways because she and Corey liked to build them out of blocks. "It's a passageway shaped like an upside down *U*." She used her hands to show Boris and Beatrice what an archway looked like.

Boris and Beatrice looked at each other and nodded. Boris bellowed, "One archway made of boulders coming right up!" Then, with huge grins, he and Beatrice began bouncing up the mountain shouting, "Attention all boulders! Wake up! It's time to build an archway over the racecourse! Get up and build an archway! I repeat! Get up and build an archway!"

Chapter Seven

As the boulders jumped and hopped toward the racecourse, Cressida and Sunbeam sprinted back to Flash, Bloom, and Ernest.

Cressida looked at Bloom and said, "Sunbeam and the boulders have agreed to help us get this cake batter off the racecourse. Bloom, will you help us, too?"

Bloom looked at Sunbeam and narrowed her eyes. "Are you sure?" she asked Sunbeam.

"I'm sure," said Sunbeam, nodding. "I'll tell you all about it later. I feel much better now. It turns out there was a bit of a misunderstanding."

Bloom shrugged. "If Sunbeam is willing to help, I am too."

Flash opened her mouth—probably to ask Sunbeam and Bloom what they were talking about—but then, thinking better of it, she just smiled, relieved her sisters were going to help save the Thunder Dash.

"Fantastic!" said Cressida. She turned around toward the racecourse, and, to her amazement, she saw that the boulders had already stacked themselves into a perfect archway that stretched the entire length of the path. "That was quick," Cressida said. "Now we have our very own, huge oven." She looked at Sunbeam. "Do you think you could shoot heat from your horn into the archway?"

Sunbeam looked hesitant. "Won't it burn the boulders?"

"The boulders love heat so much they spend every night jumping in and out of bonfires," Cressida explained.

Flash nodded. "I promise you won't hurt them."

"Well, I'll give it a try!" said Sunbeam. She walked over to the racecourse, pointed her horn toward the inside of the archway, and shot out a golden beam of light and heat.

The boulders immediately cheered. "This is great!" Boris yelled. "It's even better than bouncing in a bonfire."

Soon enough, the batter darkened to a deeper shade of pink and began to rise. When it turned golden at the top, Cressida said, "Okay, Sunbeam! I think that's enough."

Sunbeam stopped the beam of yellow light coming from her horn. "I've never baked a cake before," she said, smiling.

Next, Cressida called out, "Thank you, boulders, for your help! That was an amazing archway! Now you can go back to your spots on the mountain."

Immediately, Boris and Beatrice began to bounce and shout, "Everyone up! Time to go home! Up up up!"

The boulders unstacked themselves, exclaiming, "That was more fun than a Boulder Smolder!" and, "We should do that again!"

Now, instead of a coating of thick, sticky, strawberry cake batter on the racecourse, there was a huge pink cake. It was the longest, thickest cake Cressida had ever seen. "Are we going to run on that?" Flash asked, sounding a little nervous. "I guess we could call the race the Cake Dash. But that name isn't very catchy."

"Nope!" said Cressida. "Bloom, do you

think you could shrink this cake, so it's small enough to move off the racecourse, but big enough for all of us to eat after the race?"

"Sure thing!" said Bloom, and she pointed her shiny green horn right at the huge pink cake. She shot out a glittery green beam of light, and almost instantly the cake began to shrink, until it was the size of a large bed.

"Could you please help me move this beautiful, strawberry cake off the race-course?" Cressida asked Ernest. The wizard-lizard rushed over, and the two of them picked up the cake and gently set it down next to the starting line.

"How about if I whip up some frosting?" said Ernest excitedly. "I think I remember the spell. It's—"

But before he could finish, Flash, Bloom, and Sunbeam all shouted, "No! No more spells!" Then they all laughed, even Ernest.

Flash leaped onto the racecourse, which was paved in glittering crushed diamonds and an occasional pink cake crumb. "Oh Cressida!" Flash called out. "Thank you! You saved the Thunder Dash!"

Chapter Eight

As all the creatures in the Rainbow Realm lined up to run in the Thunder Dash, Cressida thought that she had never seen such a colorful crowd. Up in front were the princess unicorns—Flash, Sunbeam, Bloom, Moon, Breeze, Prism, and Firefly—stretching their legs and striking their hooves against the ground. Behind them, running in place and touching their toes, were throngs of foxes, rabbits, mountain goats, squirrels, cats, skunks, lizards, frogs, and turtles, all in vibrant colors—teal, green, red, purple, pink, magenta, neon orange, blue, and black. At the back were strangely colored spiders, ants, bees, slugs, snails, butterflies, and grasshoppers. Cressida even spotted several fairies beating their filmy wings, and a small herd of miniature dragons puffing fire as they stretched their legs.

Cressida found her silver unicorn sneakers next to a pine tree near the base of the racecourse. She pulled off her glittery boots, wishing she could take them home with her, and put on her running shoes. Then she took her place behind the starting line next to the unicorns, even though she knew as soon as the race started, they would run far ahead of her.

Flash climbed onto Beatrice, who sat next to the starting line smiling sleepily. "Attention!" Flash called out. "Attention!"

The crowd quieted.

"It's my honor to welcome all of you to the annual Thunder Dash!"

The crowd cheered.

"This is a very special year," Flash continued. "For the first time, we've opened up the race to all the creatures in the Rainbow Realm. And that includes our very first human girl runner, Cressida Jenkins." The crowd clapped and cheered even more loudly, and Cressida's heart fluttered in her chest. Flash winked at Cressida before she yelled, "When Beatrice bellows, the race will begin!" The crowd quieted. Flash climbed off the boulder and took her place behind the starting line.

"Go!" Beatrice bellowed, so loudly Cressida jumped in surprise.

Immediately, the princess unicorns bolted forward, their metallic hooves a blur against the crushed diamond path. Flash pulled into the lead. Behind her were Prism, Breeze, Moon, and Firefly. And behind them were Bloom and Sunbeam. All around Cressida were jogging creatures. Ernest sprinted by her, his purple hat bobbing as his blue, gold-winged sneakers carried him forward. Foxes in green

sneakers, including Felicity and Felix, passed Cressida. A rainbow-colored cat trotted by, proudly twitching her tail. Cressida, in her silver sneakers, was glad that she was at least faster than the turtles, the spiders, the ants, and the grasshoppers.

The boulders, lined up along the race-course, cheered on the runners.

Just when Cressida was starting to lose her breath, and her legs were starting to get tired, she saw the finish line ahead. With her heart thundering in her chest, she pushed herself to run as fast as she could. With every last bit of energy, she sprinted to the finish line, leaping across as her sneakers blinked.

At the top of the mountain, Cressida

gulped down two cups of water and found the unicorns standing by a silver trough. Flash, as always, had won the race, and she wore a gold medal. Prism, who had come in second, wore a silver medal. Breeze, wearing a bronze medal, had finished third.

"Congratulations!" Cressida said, looking at Flash, Prism, and Breeze. Then she looked at Sunbeam.

"Guess what?" Sunbeam said to Cressida. "I ran the fastest I've ever run before. I had my best time yet. I think it was because I could hear Boris and Beatrice cheering me on. They told me I looked sunny!"

"Wow! That's great!" Cressida said.

"I'm very proud of my littlest sister," Flash said. "This really is my favorite day of the year. Thank you, Cressida, for being the very first human girl to run in the

Thunder Dash. It's been our honor to have you."

"It's been my honor to run," said Cressida, grabbing another cup of water. She didn't think she had ever run so fast or so hard in her life.

"I know you'll need to go home soon," Flash said, and Cressida nodded. She had to admit she was tired and ready to see her parents and Corey. "But before you go, please have a piece of cake. Boris bounced it all the way up to the finish line so we could enjoy it."

Ernest, still wearing his blue winged shoes, jogged over to Cressida. He held two forks and two plates of strawberry cake, each piled high with the brightest yellow frosting Cressida had ever seen. "I couldn't help myself. A cake needs frosting!" Ernest said, blushing.

"Thank you," said Cressida, and she began to cut off a small bite of cake with her fork.

Ernest shoveled a huge mound of pink cake and yellow frosting into his scaly mouth, and then his face fell. "Oh dear! You better not eat that."

"Why not?" Cressida asked, putting down her fork.

Ernest smiled sheepishly. "Well, I meant to make cranberry-flavored frosting, but it seems I made canary-flavored frosting by accident. I feel like I have a mouth full of feathers. Don't worry. There were no real canaries involved."

Cressida began to giggle. "Oh Ernest," she said. "Don't worry about it."

Just then, Cressida's stomach rumbled. But what she really wanted to eat, instead of cake, was a peanut butter and banana sandwich, some carrot sticks with hummus, blueberry yogurt, and maybe, if she was still hungry after all that, an apple.

Flash caught Cressida's eye and walked over. "You look like you might be about ready to go back to the human world," she said.

"Well," Cressida said. "It's true I'd like to eat some human food. And I miss my parents and Corey."

Flash nodded. "It was a pleasure to have you as our guest in the Rainbow Realm. Thank you so much for saving the Thunder Dash."

"I had such a great time today," said Cressida. "Thank you so much for inviting me!"

Flash, Sunbeam, Bloom, Prism, Firefly, Moon, and Breeze surrounded Cressida. "Thank you so much for coming!" they called out. "Come back soon!"

"And remember," Sunbeam said, "you're welcome back anytime. And when we want to signal for you to visit us for a special reason, we'll make your key turn bright pink. Do you promise you won't forget?"

Cressida laughed at the idea that she

could ever forget. "I promise," said Cressida. With that, Cressida pulled her key from her pocket and put both hands on the crystal handle. "Take me home, please!" Cressida said. The Thunder Peaks began to spin and spin into a quickening blur of silver, gold, copper, and bronze. Cressida felt as though she were soaring through the air, higher and higher. And then, with a gentle *thud*, she found herself sitting at the base of the oak tree in the woods behind her house. Cressida stood up slowly and smiled. She was wearing her rainbow leggings and her blue unicorn sweater again. But she felt something heavy and unfamiliar around her neck. She looked down, and there hung a gold medal with pink sequins.

On the front was a picture of a running unicorn. And on the back, in engraved letters,

it said, CRESSIDA JENKINS, FIRST HUMAN GIRL TO RUN IN THE THUNDER DASH.

Cressida smiled. And then, though her legs were tired, Cressida ran home, her sneakers blinking and her medal swinging across her chest.

Unicorn Princesses
BLOOM'S BALL

Chapter One

In the top tower of Spiral Palace, Ernest, a wizard-lizard wearing a purple pointy hat and a matching cape, put three apricots on a chair. Above him, two tomatoes, each with bright yellow wings, swooped down from a bookshelf. Near the window, three silver-winged bananas hovered. A flock of plums fluttered their gold wings around a chandelier.

Ernest cleared his throat and raised his wand. But as he opened his mouth to begin casting a spell, he heard a knock on the door. "Come in!" he called out.

The door opened, and in stepped Princess Bloom, a mint-green unicorn with a magic emerald that hung around her neck on a purple ribbon. In her mouth, she carried a blue velvet bag. Bloom smiled as she admired Ernest's flying tomatoes, bananas, and plums. Then she dropped the bag between her shiny green hooves and said, "You sure have been working hard on your flying spells. It looks like you've finally gotten the hang of it."

Ernest blushed. "I've been practicing for weeks," he said. "At the beginning, all the fruits and vegetables grew springs instead of wings. There were oranges and peaches bouncing and boinging all over the room. But now they sprout wings, usually on my first or second try."

Just then, a swooping tomato collided with a plum right above Ernest's head. With a *splat*, the tomato landed on the pointed tip of Ernest's hat. "Not again," he groaned as red juice dripped into his eyes.

Bloom giggled.

"Anyway," Ernest said, wiping his face with his cape, "what brings you to my tower?"

"I was wondering," Bloom said, "if you might use your magic to help me."

Ernest grinned with delight. The unicorn princesses often teased him about his spells, which usually seemed to go wrong. It was unusual for a creature in the Rainbow Realm to ask for his magical assistance. "I'd be most honored," he said, dabbing a final drop of tomato juice from his long, green nose.

Bloom opened the velvet bag and pulled out a stack of lime-colored, glittery envelopes. "These are invitations to my birthday party this afternoon," she explained. "I'm about to take them to the mail-snails to deliver. But there's one invitation I wanted to send in a special way." Bloom passed an especially glittery envelope to Ernest. On the front, it said,

To My Sister and Best Friend,
Princess Prism

"As you know," Bloom continued, "Prism likes anything that's playful and creative. And she loves surprises. I was wondering if you could cast a spell on the invitation so it grows wings and flies to her."

"Absolutely!" Ernest exclaimed, jumping up and down. "And I know exactly which spell to use. It's in my favorite book, *Wings on Things,* volume three. Or is it volume two?" Ernest scratched his forehead.

A look of concern crossed Bloom's face. "Are you absolutely sure you can do it?"

"Oh yes!" Ernest said. "I promise I won't make any mistakes."

"In that case," said Bloom, "thank you so much for your help. And now I'd better hurry to take the rest of the invitations to the mail-snails. If I don't drop them off now, the mail-snails won't have enough time to deliver them before the party starts." She smiled sheepishly. "You know me! I have trouble doing almost anything before the last minute." With that, Bloom pushed the rest of the envelopes back into the velvet bag, grabbed the sack in her mouth, and rushed out the door.

As soon as Bloom was gone, Ernest raced over to a bookshelf and pulled down a thick, black book. He flipped through the pages and stopped on page 147. Rubbing his scaly hands together, he exclaimed, "Bloom and Prism will love this!"

He put Prism's invitation on the table. He picked up his wand. And he chanted, "Happety Bappety Birthday Bloom! Wingety Swingety Fluttery Sloom! Glittery Flittery Slittery Sail! Prettily Flittery Slittery Quail!"

Ernest waited. Nothing happened. The envelope didn't even jump or tremble, and there certainly weren't any wings—or even springs—growing from it.

"Oh dear!" Ernest said, hitting his forehead with his palm. "Did I say 'quail' instead of 'mail'? Oh dear!"

Just then, thunder rumbled, and Ernest sprinted to the window in time to see several bolts of purple light flashing in the distance.

"Not again," Ernest groaned. "Hopefully, nothing will go wrong until after Bloom's party."

He shrugged and returned to the envelope. He checked the book again. And then he waved his wand and chanted, "Happety Bappety Birthday Bloom! Wingety Swingety Fluttery Sloom! Glittery Flittery Slittery Sail! Prettily Flittery Slittery Mail!" This time, the invitation spun around and two tiny, sparkling green wings sprouted from one of its corners. "Oh dear," Ernest said. "Those wings are awfully small."

The envelope flapped its wings and rose a few inches into the air. "Well, at least it can fly," Ernest said, shrugging. He carried the envelope to the open window. "Off you go to Princess Prism," he said. The envelope jumped off his hand and began to flutter, ever so slowly, down the side of Spiral Palace.

Chapter Two

Cressida Jenkins sat at her family's kitchen table with a pink pen and a stack of cards, each with a picture of a unicorn leaping over a rainbow on the front. She was writing thank-you notes to her friends who had come to her birthday celebration that past weekend. Her party had been wonderful: there had been unicorn-shaped balloons, unicorn cupcakes, a unicorn piñata, and a game of pin-the-tail-on-the-unicorn. Her friends had given her two stuffed unicorns, unicorn socks, a unicorn poster, a unicorn board game, four books about unicorns that weren't in her school's library, and a unicorn necklace.

Cressida decided to write her first thank-you note to her friend Daphne, who had given her the necklace. She wrote, "Dear Daphne," inside one of the cards. She wanted to mention, in her note, how much she loved the color of the unicorn charm, but she suddenly couldn't remember whether it was silver or gold. She was almost positive it was gold, but she wanted to check. Cressida got up from her chair and dashed down the hall to her room. She

found the necklace dangling from one of the hooks in her closet. Sure enough, a gold unicorn hung from a rainbow ribbon. She smiled, thinking about Daphne, who had a matching one. She picked up the necklace and put it around her neck. Maybe she and Daphne were now wearing their unicorn necklaces at the same time!

Just as Cressida was about to return to the kitchen, she heard a tinkling noise, like something between a harp and one of the triangles she played in music class at school. Cressida's heart skipped a beat, and an enormous smile spread across her face. She bounded over to her bedside table, opened the drawer, and pulled out an old-fashioned key with a crystal ball for a handle. The handle glowed bright pink and pulsed. The unicorn princesses were inviting her to the Rainbow Realm!

Cressida had first visited the Rainbow Realm and met the unicorn princesses after she found a similar key—old-fashioned, with a crystal-ball handle—on a walk through the woods with her parents and her older brother, Corey. Later, worried the key's owner might be looking for it, she returned it to the forest to discover the key belonged to a yellow unicorn named Princess Sunbeam. Cressida traveled with Sunbeam back to the Rainbow Realm, an enchanted world ruled by seven royal unicorn sisters. There, Cressida met all six of Sunbeam's siblings: silver Princess

Flash, green Princess Bloom, purple Princess Prism, black Princess Moon, blue Princess Breeze, and orange Princess Firefly. Each unicorn princess ruled over her own domain within the Rainbow Realm and wore a gemstone necklace that gave her unique magic powers. Cressida became such good friends with the unicorns that they gave her a key of her own. They told her she was welcome to visit any time, and that if they ever wanted to invite her back for a special occasion, the key's handle would glow bright pink.

Now, Cressida put the glowing, tinkling key in her jeans pocket. She slid her feet into her silver unicorn sneakers, which had pink lights that blinked every time she walked, ran, or jumped. She hurried into the kitchen, where she ate a blueberry granola bar in three big bites and gulped down a glass of water. Then, she called out to her mother, who was working at her computer in the living room, "I'm going for a quick walk in the woods."

"Okay, honey. Just make sure you finish your thank-you notes today," her mother called back.

"I promise I will," Cressida said. "I'll be back soon." Time in the human world froze while Cressida was in the Rainbow Realm, so she really would be back soon, even if she spent hours with the unicorns.

Cressida ran through her family's small backyard and into the woods behind her house. She raced down her favorite path, her sneakers blinking, until she came to a gigantic oak tree. She kneeled next to the tree and pushed her key into the tiny hole near the roots. Cressida grinned, giddy with excitement, as the forest began to spin, first becoming a blur of green and brown and then turning pitch black. Cressida suddenly felt as though she were falling through space, and she smiled, knowing that in a few seconds she would see the unicorn princesses.

With a gentle *thud*, Cressida landed on something soft. At first, all she could see was a swirl of silver, white, pink, and purple. But soon the room stopped spinning, and she found herself on an enormous lavender armchair. Crystal chandeliers hung from the ceilings. The scents of vanilla and cedar floated in the air. Pink and purple velvet curtains blew in the breeze. Cressida smiled. She was in the front room of Spiral Palace, the unicorn princesses' giant, shimmering, horn-shaped home.

ressida heard the clatter of hooves on the tile floors. And then, in front of her stood all seven unicorn princesses. The magic gemstones on their necklaces glittered in the light of the chandeliers.

"My human girl is back!" called out Sunbeam. She twirled and then jumped into the air, clicking her gold hooves together.

Flash flicked her mane and grinned.

Prism swished her tail and winked at Cressida.

"Welcome back, Cressida," said Breeze, Firefly, and Moon in unison.

Bloom trotted up to Cressida and gushed, "Thank you so much for coming! I was hoping you'd be able to make the trip to the Rainbow Realm this afternoon."

"Bloom insisted we invite you here," Sunbeam explained, "but she wouldn't tell us why."

"She says it's a surprise," Flash added.

"Bloom's my best friend, and she won't even tell me what the surprise is!" Prism said.

"But whatever it is," Moon added, "we're thrilled you're here."

"I couldn't be happier to be here," Cressida said. "I can't wait to find out about Bloom's surprise."

Just then, Cressida heard a high-pitched sound. She turned toward the palace door to see a teal chipmunk wearing a red uniform and blowing into a bugle. Behind the chipmunk were six giant orange snails, and attached to each enormous snail shell was a green, glittery envelope. The snails' antennae twitched as they fanned out across the room, and Cressida noticed a snail was headed straight toward each of the unicorns except Bloom and Prism. And then, to her delight, Cressida realized one snail was gliding toward her!

The snail stopped in front of Cressida and said, in a squeaky voice, "Cressida Jenkins, I presume?"

"That's me!"

"I've got a special snail-mail delivery for you," the snail squeaked.

"Thank you," Cressida said, carefully pulling the glittery green envelope off the snail's shell. She read these words, in lime-green writing, on the front:

To: Cressida Jenkins,
My Favorite Human Girl
From: Princess Bloom

The snail winked at Cressida, twirled her antennae, and slid away. Cressida opened the envelope and pulled out a card with an orange flower on the front. Inside, it read:

You are cordially invited to a
Birthday Garden Ball
for Princess Bloom this afternoon
in the Enchanted Garden.

Cressida's heart swelled with excitement. She wasn't completely sure what a garden ball was, but any kind of birthday celebration with real unicorns sounded even more fun than her own birthday party had been.

Cressida looked up to see Flash, Sunbeam, Breeze, Moon, and Firefly opening their cards. But Prism, who hadn't received one, frowned as she watched the fleet of mail-snails gliding out of the palace. Cressida wondered why Prism hadn't gotten an invitation, especially since Prism and Bloom were best friends. She couldn't imagine Bloom would exclude Prism, and she hoped a mail-snail with a card for Prism would arrive soon.

Bloom bounded over to Cressida. "Surprise!" the unicorn sang out. "The reason I invited you to the Rainbow Realm was so you could join me for my birthday garden ball. So, can you come?"

"Absolutely!" said Cressida. "I can't wait! But I have one question: What, exactly, is a garden ball?"

"I was wondering the same thing," Sunbeam said.

"Me too," Flash and Firefly said at once.

"Well," began Bloom, smiling proudly, "it's a special kind of party I made up! I love garden parties because they're outside, there's always good food, and they're not too formal. But there's never enough dancing! And I love balls because there's lots of dancing. But, to be honest, I don't always like wearing a scratchy, formal cape for hours on end. And I usually spend the whole ball feeling a little hungry because there's never very much food. So I thought I'd celebrate my birthday with the best parts of each and call it a garden ball. It will be outside with amazing food and lots of dancing. But no formal capes are allowed!"

"A garden ball," Breeze said. "What a great idea."

"That's a perfect kind of party for you," Moon said.

Cressida jumped up and down with excitement. And then she looked down at her clothes. The left knee of her jeans was torn from a time she had tripped while playing freeze-tag in the backyard with Corey. And, even worse, the front of her green T-shirt had a stain that looked like it was either from spaghetti sauce or red paint. The only thing she was wearing that looked even remotely appropriate for any kind of party was the unicorn necklace

Daphne had given her. "I'm not dressed for a garden ball," Cressida said, frowning.

"I'll fix that!" called out a high, nasal voice. Ernest jogged into the room clutching his wand.

"Hello, Ernest," Cressida said.

"I've been working on this spell for the past hour," Ernest announced, breathless. "Watch this!" He waved his wand and chanted, "Pinkery Puffery Dressery Droo! Dottily Spottily Puffily Foo!"

Wind swirled around Cressida. Then, suddenly, she was wearing a bright pink dress with white polka dots and the puffiest skirt she had ever seen. On her feet were black, shiny Mary Jane shoes. "Well?" Ernest asked excitedly. "What do you think?"

The dress felt stiff and itchy. And the shoes pinched Cressida's toes and seemed much too uncomfortable for running and jumping. Cressida decided to be honest. "It was very thoughtful of you to make this dress and these shoes for me," she said. "But they're not exactly my style."

"That's true," said Ernest, nodding. "Honestly, I'm just excited the dress came out with dots instead of pots. A dress with metal pots all over it is heavy. And noisy, too, with all that clanging. Let me try another one!"

Cressida laughed and tried not to scratch her legs, which felt itchier and itchier the longer she wore the dress's puffy skirt.

Ernest cleared his throat. He lifted his wand. And he chanted, "Greenily Sparkily

Lemmings Loo! Birthday Dressily Purple Ploo!"

Cressida felt another rush of wind. When she looked down, she was wearing purple sneakers and a bright purple party dress that was exactly right for her: it had big pockets, and it was comfortable enough for running, jumping, climbing, and dancing. But now she was back to wearing her torn jeans underneath the dress. And at her feet sat what looked like five green, glittery rodents.

"Are those mice?" Cressida asked, taking a step backward. She was pleased to notice her new sneakers had green lights that blinked when she stepped.

One of the little animals looked up and rolled her eyes. "Everyone always thinks we're mice. But we're *lemmings*. L-E-M-M-I-N-G-S! We're rodents that live in very cold places, like the Arctic. And, I must say, we usually don't look like we've been to a Saint Patrick's Day parade! In fact," the lemming sniffed, "we lemmings have refused to celebrate Saint Patrick's Day ever since a leprechaun had the nerve to call us rats!"

"Oh dear!" Ernest said. "Did I say *lemmings* again? I meant *leggings*. Let me fix that!"

Cressida giggled as Ernest waved his wand and chanted, "Greenily Sparkily Leggings Loo! Send the Lemmings Back Home, Too!"

In one last burst of wind, the lemmings vanished. When Cressida looked down, green, glittery leggings had replaced her jeans. "Thanks so much, Ernest!" she said, spinning around. "This is perfect!" She touched her hand to her chest, and, to her relief, her unicorn necklace was still there, under her dress.

Ernest blushed and took a bow.

"What a great outfit," said Bloom. "And now that you're perfectly dressed for a garden ball, want to come with me to the Enchanted Garden to help me finish getting ready?"

"I'd love to!" replied Cressida.

Just then, Sunbeam looked at Bloom and smiled teasingly. "It's just like you to send out your invitations on the very same day as your party! How did you know we wouldn't already have other plans this afternoon?"

"We love our sister Bloom, but she always does everything at the very last minute," Flash explained to Cressida. "And sometimes she even does things *after* the last minute. There was one year when she held her party after her actual birthday because she couldn't get ready in time."

Prism swished her tail and frowned. She looked like she wanted to defend her best friend, but she wasn't sure what to say, given that she still hadn't received an invitation.

Bloom smiled, but Cressida could see the unicorn felt hurt. "Sure, I should have sent out the invitations earlier," Bloom said. "But wait until you see the garden ball I have planned!"

"Planned? I'll believe that when I see it!" Sunbeam said. "But seriously, Bloom, we're all thrilled to come to your garden ball. Luckily, my only plans this afternoon were to sunbathe and to roll around in a patch of purple clover in the Glitter Canyon. I can most certainly reschedule that for tomorrow afternoon."

"Cressida is coming with me to the Enchanted Garden to finish getting ready for the garden ball," Bloom said. "We'll see you in just two hours." Then she kneeled, and Cressida climbed onto the unicorn's back. She held onto Bloom's mane, wavy and shiny like Easter-basket grass, and the unicorn turned and trotted toward the door.

Just then, Cressida heard Firefly say, "Don't worry, Prism. I bet the mail-snail delivering your invitation just took an extra-long lunch break or had to stop at the shell repair shop. I'm sure your invitation will be here in no time."

Chapter Four

Cressida felt giddy with excitement as she rode Bloom out of Spiral Palace and along the clear stones that led into the surrounding forest. She couldn't wait to see the Enchanted Garden or to celebrate Bloom's birthday.

"My sisters always tease me about waiting until the last minute," Bloom said as she came to a cluster of pine trees and turned left onto a wide, flat path. "But guess what? I've been planning this party for weeks. I've already baked a clover cake, churned dandelion ice cream, and grown a huge harvest of fruit just for the occasion. This morning, the orchard gnomes helped me blow up balloons and hang streamers. The only thing left to do is make the goody bags. And I was thinking you could help me since you have hands instead of hooves."

"Wow! Your garden ball sounds great," Cressida said, hoping she would get to meet the orchard gnomes. "And I'd be glad to help with the goody bags. Having hands is, well, awfully handy sometimes."

Bloom giggled at Cressida's joke. "I know my sisters aren't expecting a very good party. I can't wait to see their faces when they see the cake, the ice cream, and all the decorations. It's true I should have sent those invitations out earlier. But every time I was about to address the envelopes, I got distracted by something that sounded more fun. Especially since I have to use my mouth to hold the pen when I write. It takes forever!"

Just then, Bloom stopped in front of a patch of bright red mushrooms with white spots. "Speaking of fun, it will only take a few minutes to make the goody bags. I think there's time to play before we get to work."

"Sounds good!" Cressida said. Bloom kneeled, and Cressida slid onto the ground.

"I'll show you one of my favorite things to do," Bloom said. "I can't pass this mushroom patch without having a little fun, even when I'm running late."

Bloom pointed her shiny green horn at the mushrooms. The emerald on her necklace twinkled. And then, a beam of sparkling green light shot out from her horn. Immediately, the mushrooms began to grow and grow. Soon, they were twice as tall as Cressida, and they filled a space three times as large as her bedroom. For a moment, Bloom paused and admired her work. Then, she pointed her horn at three of the giant mushrooms and shrank them, one by one, so the first was Cressida's height, the second came up to her waist, and the third reached her knees. They looked, Cressida thought, like a staircase.

Bloom turned to Cressida and grinned. "Ready?" she asked. And then, before Cressida could respond, she bounded up the mushroom staircase and began to jump, soaring higher and higher into the sky. Bloom had just created the biggest trampoline Cressida had ever seen.

Cressida followed Bloom up the staircase. At the top, she smiled at the huge, spongy, red floor with white spots before she stepped to the center of the mushroom trampoline and jumped. "Wheeee!" she called out as she flew into the air. The trampoline was even bouncier than the one in Daphne's backyard.

"I told you this would be fun!" Bloom called out, hopping toward Cressida and launching herself into the air.

Cressida and Bloom squealed as they jumped and jumped, each time soaring higher and higher.

"Watch this!" Bloom said. "I've been practicing this trick for the past few months!" Then, on a particularly high bounce, Bloom somersaulted and landed on her hooves.

"Wow!" Cressida said, clapping.

"You try it!" Bloom sang out as she did two more flips in the air.

Cressida bent her knees and jumped as high as she could. She bounced three more times, each time flying higher and higher.

And then, on her fifth jump, she tucked her knees to her chest and somersaulted. To her amazement, she landed on her feet.

"Well done!" Bloom said. "I'd give that a perfect ten!"

"Thank you!" Cressida said, giggling. She took a bow.

Cressida and Bloom both did several more somersaults before Bloom said, "Do you think we should head to the Enchanted Garden? I could stay here all day, but my sisters will make fun of me if we're still putting together the goody bags when they arrive."

"Sure," Cressida said. She didn't feel like getting off the trampoline, but she wanted to make sure Bloom was ready for her garden ball before her guests arrived.

"I'm going to do one more flip!" Bloom said. "Well, actually two. I'm going to make this one a double!" And then she soared up into the air, did two somersaults, and landed on her back hooves.

"Amazing!" Cressida said.

"Do you think there's time to do just a few more somersaults?" Bloom asked.

Cressida giggled at her friend. She could see exactly how Bloom had earned her reputation for waiting until the last minute. "I have an idea," Cressida said. "How about if we go to the Enchanted Garden now, put together your goody bags, and make sure everything is completely ready. And if we finish before it's time for your garden ball, we can come back and jump some more."

Bloom nodded. "Sounds like a plan."

Bloom bounded over to the mushroom staircase, hopped down, and waited as Cressida followed her to the ground. The earth under Cressida's feet felt strangely hard and solid compared to the mushroom trampoline.

Bloom pointed her horn at the mushrooms and said, "Move out of the way! I don't want to accidentally shrink you."

Cressida quickly stepped backward as Bloom shot a green, glittery beam of light at the mushrooms until they shrank to their normal size.

"You know," said Bloom, winking, "I was just teasing about shrinking you. My magic works on objects and plants, but not on other animals." The unicorn kneeled down so Cressida could climb onto her back.

"I can't wait to see the Enchanted Garden," Cressida said.

"We're almost there," Bloom said, and she took a sharp right onto a narrow path that ended at a tall, white stone wall with an iron gate. At the top of the gate were the words, "Enchanted Garden," written in emeralds.

"Close your eyes!" Bloom called out. Cressida shut her eyes. She heard the gate open, and she felt Bloom take several steps forward. "All righty!" said Bloom. "Now you can look!"

Chapter Five

Cressida opened her eyes to see rows and rows of trees, all with leaves that looked like pieces of emerald-colored foil. "Welcome to the orchard," Bloom said as she kneeled, and Cressida slid onto the ground. "This is where I grow all the fruit my sisters and I eat."

Hanging from the branches were fruits in every color and shape Cressida could imagine. Some were fruits she recognized from the human world: apples, oranges, peaches, plums, apricots, and nectarines. She also spotted several purple-and-pink-striped roinkleberries, the sweet fruit she had eaten during her first visit to the Rainbow Realm. But most of the branches were covered in fruit she had never seen before. Shiny orange-and-blue-striped fruit cascaded in bunches like giant grapes. Red fruit with yellow spots, and yellow fruit with red spots, dangled on long, thick stems. Pink and purple fruit that looked like glittery rubber balls dotted some of the branches.

And bunches of teal, banana-like fruit swayed in the light breeze. Most of the trees held elaborate wooden birdhouses, each with several floors and entrances. Tiny bluebirds flew in and out of them, swooping from tree to tree.

Cressida noticed that nearly everywhere she looked, there were garden gnomes wearing pointy red hats and brown work boots. They were climbing up and down ladders as they filled small wooden baskets with picked fruit. They were watering the trees with purple garden hoses. And they were busily working with hammers and nails to build ladders, fruit baskets, birdhouses, benches, tables, and chairs.

"Are those the orchard gnomes?" Cressida asked. She tried not to stare, though she couldn't help herself.

"They sure are," Bloom said. "They love to garden. They pick all the fruit, water and prune the trees, and take care of the birds. Another thing about gnomes is they love building things out of wood. They spend all their spare time making furniture."

Just then, two gnomes marched over to Cressida and Bloom carrying a wooden basket. "Salutations!" they said in unison. "My name is Gnorbert," one of them said, "and this is Gnatasha."

"It's a pleasure to meet you," Cressida said, bending over to shake the gnomes' hands. "I'm Cressida Jenkins. I'm here for Bloom's birthday garden ball."

"Splendid!" the gnomes said.

"We were wondering if you might like to try some fruit," Gnatasha explained. "Nearly all the ripe fruit is already in troughs for Bloom's party. But I happen to have right here a fresh cranglenapple." She handed Cressida a shiny red fruit with yellow spots. "And this froyanana is perfectly ripe." She gave Cressida one of the teal bananas.

"Thank you!" Cressida said.

"You're most welcome," said Gnorbert. "We'd better get back to work. We're about to build a brand new bench."

"And a huge castle for the bluebirds," Gnatasha added, pulling a small hammer from her tool belt and twirling it in her fingers. The two gnomes marched off, whistling.

Bloom glanced at Cressida. "Which are you going to eat first?"

Cressida looked at the two fruits, and her stomach growled. She decided to start with the cranglenapple. She took a bite of the red-and-yellow fruit, and laughed as pink juice dripped down her chin. It tasted like a mix of watermelon, cotton candy, and mint bubble gum. "This is really good!" she said, taking several more bites to finish the cranglenapple.

"They're my second favorite," confessed Bloom. "What I really love are froyananas."

Cressida unpeeled the froyanana to find inside what looked like a magenta banana with violet stripes. Bloom smiled. "I could eat those all day long."

Cressida took a bite, and tried not to gag. It tasted like combination of pickles, marshmallows, tomatoes, and tuna fish. "I don't think this one is for me," she said, wishing she could drink some water to get the terrible taste out of her mouth.

"I'll finish it for you!" Bloom said, and ate the rest in one bite. "This one is awfully mild. Want me to see if the gnomes can find one with a stronger flavor? Maybe then you'd like it more."

"Um, no, thank you," Cressida said quickly. "I've had enough froyanana for now. I'm really not hungry anymore."

"Maybe later," Bloom suggested.

"Maybe," Cressida said, though she was quite certain she would not. She decided she would rather eat three bowls of lima beans and frozen peas—her two least favorite foods—than one more bite of froyanana.

Bloom shrugged. "Come this way, and I'll show you the vegetables," she said. Cressida followed Bloom along a row of plum trees, through a cluster of trees with ruby-red fruit the size of soccer balls, and around five gnomes building a miniature Spiral Palace for the bluebirds.

On the far side of the orchard, Bloom led Cressida through a gated wooden fence and into a vegetable garden that was the size of three classrooms at Cressida's elementary school. There were rows of plants Cressida knew from her school's garden—carrots, corn, eggplant, zucchini, tomatoes, peppers, pumpkins, yellow squash, and sugar snap peas. And then there were vegetables Cressida had never seen: purple vines with teal vegetables that looked like starfish, stout pink plants with yellow berries, and red bushes covered in white-and-black, bagel-shaped vegetables. But the strangest thing Cressida noticed were piles of small yellow dragons, each with a set of folded wings, sleeping among the vegetables.

"What are those?" Cressida said.

"Those are the mini-dragons," Bloom explained. "They're the sleepiest creatures in the Rainbow Realm." Just then, several lizards, asleep in a nearby pile, stirred and then began to snore. "The only way to

get them to wake up is to show them something metal and shiny. They love silver and gold. But other than that, forget it! They just nap all day long."

Bloom noticed a cluster of weeds by her front hooves. She pointed her horn downward. The magic emerald on her necklace glittered before she shot a green beam of light at the weeds. Almost instantly, they shrank until they were so small Cressida couldn't see them.

"I'll do more weeding later," Bloom said. "Right now, we'd better head over to the flower garden to finish making those goody bags. I can't wait to show you the cake, the ice cream, the troughs of fruit, and all the decorations. This is going to be the best birthday party my sisters have ever seen."

Bloom led Cressida to the far side of the vegetable patch, where they came to a high stone wall with a wooden gate. "Get ready!" Bloom said, and she pushed open the gate with her hoof.

Chapter Six

As soon as Bloom opened the gate, she gasped. In the walled-off flower garden, perched on the sides of all the gold and silver troughs of fruit, clustered on the wooden benches, strutting along the brick paths, and digging through the flower beds, were orange quail with lime-green eyes. Quail nibbled on Bloom's five-tiered, green and yellow cake, eating the frosting and chewing on the candles. Quail pecked hungrily at the light-green ice cream in silver buckets. Quail clustered around two large harps, using their beaks and talons to yank on the strings until they snapped in two. Quail wrapped themselves in streamers and popped balloons. A few quail even wore birthday hats. All the while, the quail excitedly repeated, "*Meep! Meep! Meep!*"

"Oh no!" whinnied Bloom. She looked at her ruined cake and blinked back tears. "How did this happen? Do you think I'll have to cancel my birthday party?"

Before Cressida could respond, three large purple earthworms, each the size of a small snake, wiggled out from a flower bed

and squirmed over to Bloom and Cressida. "We're sorry about the quail," one of them said.

"We tried to stop them," the second explained.

"But they wouldn't listen," said the third.

The first worm looked at Cressida and said, "My name is Wilhelmina. And this is Wallaby." She nodded toward the second worm. "And here's Worthington." She pointed her tail toward the third worm.

"I'm Cressida Jenkins," Cressida said.

"How did all these quail get here?" Bloom asked, frowning as a bird jumped from balloon to balloon, loudly popping each one.

"We were burrowing through the dirt, as usual," Worthington explained. "We'd found a great spot by those rosebushes. Then, all of a sudden, we heard thunder and saw purple lightning. The next thing we knew, there were quail everywhere."

"We asked them to go somewhere else," Wilhelmina said.

"We asked nicely at first. And then we were pretty rude," Wallaby added. "But instead of leaving, they um, well—" His voice trailed off.

"What Wallaby is too polite to say," Worthington explained, "is that they tried to eat us! It turns out the only food quail like more than cake, ice cream, and fruit is earthworm. We've been hiding in that bed of tulips ever since. The only reason they haven't already eaten us is, well, they aren't very smart."

Bloom sighed heavily. "Oh, I knew I shouldn't have trusted Ernest with that invitation."

"What invitation?" Cressida asked.

"I'll tell you later," said Bloom. "Right now we need to get the quail out of here before they start eating the rest of the Enchanted Garden. It's bad enough to lose everything I cooked and made and grew for my party. But it would be much worse to lose all the other fruits and vegetables. Then what would my sisters and I eat? Plus, we certainly don't want the quail to eat the earthworms!"

Bloom walked to the center of the flock of quail. She cleared her throat to get their attention, but they continued gnawing on candles, pecking at the cake, and wrapping themselves in party streamers. Two quail, perched on the side of an ice cream bucket, jumped in and covered their feathers in the cold, green dessert, squealing, *"Meep! Meep! Meep!"* Three other quail found a cluster of balloons behind a rosebush and popped them with their beaks. Then they played tug-of-war with the deflated balloons. Bloom stomped her hoof, but the quail still didn't look up. Finally, she whistled so loudly Cressida covered her ears.

"Attention all quail!" Bloom called out. "It's time for you to leave the Enchanted

Garden! Please fly over that wall immediately!" Bloom pointed with her horn to the far wall of the flower garden. Finally, the birds stopped pecking and playing. They stared at Bloom and blinked their green eyes. Several cocked their heads and tweeted, "*Meep?*" And then, to Cressida's dismay, they shrugged and carried on eating the party food and playing with the decorations.

Bloom looked at Cressida and frowned. "Can you think of any other way to get them out of here?"

Cressida scratched her head. And then, she had an idea. It was a strange idea. But she was pretty sure it would work.

"I think so," Cressida said, going over the details of her plan in her head. "Bloom, would you mind staying here and making sure the quail don't eat Wallaby, Wilhelmina, and Worthington while I ask the gnomes a question?"

Bloom nodded. "You always have the most creative ideas," she said. "I'll be right here, protecting the worms."

Cressida sprinted out of the flower garden, through the rows of vegetables, and back to the orchard. She spotted Gnorbert and Gnatasha under a tree building a bench. Cressida jogged over to them.

Gnorbert looked up at her and smiled. He had several nails in his mouth, and was holding a hammer. Gnatasha, busy measuring a piece of wood, barely glanced up as she asked, "How can we help you?"

"Well," said Cressida, realizing her request might sound strange, "I'm wondering if you could please build me a quail roost. And it would be good if it weren't very heavy."

Cressida waited for Gnatasha and Gnorbert to ask her why she would possibly want a quail roost, but Gnorbert said, "How many quail will need to roost on it?"

"Twenty. Or maybe twenty-five," Cressida said.

Gnatasha and Gnorbert nodded and said, in unison, "One lightweight, medium-size quail roost coming up!" They immediately began gathering wooden beams from nearby piles of wood and taking measurements with the rulers they kept behind their pointed ears. As Gnatasha started hammering, Gnorbert dashed into a shed and reappeared with three teetering stacks of nests made of blue straw.

In almost no time, Gnatasha and Gnorbert were standing on either side of what looked like a tall bookcase with a neat row of nests on each shelf. "Amazing!" Cressida said. "Thank you!" She tried to lift the roost, expecting it to be heavy. But she found she could easily carry it.

"How did you make this so light?" Cressida asked.

Gnatasha winked. Gnorbert said, "We gnomes are a little bit magic." And then they both bowed before they hurried back to building their bench.

Cressida carried the roost through the orchard and into the vegetable garden. She paused and surveyed the piles of sleeping mini-dragons, trying to decide which ones looked friendliest. Finally, she approached two sleeping in a ball beneath a bush covered with what looked like orange-and-pink-polka-dotted zucchini.

"Excuse me," Cressida said. "I'm sorry to bother you." One of the mini-dragons half-opened her eyes. "My name is Cressida. I'm friends with Bloom."

"I'm Drusilla," the mini-dragon said, stretching. "This is my brother Drudwyn." Drudwyn blinked and yawned.

For a moment, Drusilla and Drudwyn stared at Cressida. Then their eyelids began to droop. Cressida could tell they were about to fall back asleep.

"I'm wondering," said Cressida, "if you could do me a favor."

"Maybe," Drusilla said, looking annoyed. "Well, honestly, probably not. How long will it take?"

"I don't really like doing work," Drudwyn added. "It's much more fun to nap."

"I know you really like to sleep," Cressida said, "but I'm wondering if you could take a short break from napping. I only need help for five or ten minutes."

Drusilla and Drudwyn whispered for a few seconds. Then, Drusilla said, "Nope. Sorry."

"But," Cressida said, "you'd be helping to save the Enchanted Garden from a flock of quail."

Drusilla and Drudwyn shook their heads. "Sorry," Drudwyn said. "No can do."

Cressida's heart sank. Then she remembered Bloom had mentioned the dragons liked shiny presents. Cressida put her hand on her chest and felt the unicorn charm under her purple dress. She didn't want to give away Daphne's present. But saving the Enchanted Garden was more important than her unicorn charm.

Cressida pulled the necklace over her head and dangled it in front of the mini-dragons. Drusilla and Drudwyn stood up, widened their eyes, and stretched their long, yellow wings. "Well, well, well," Drusilla said, not taking her eyes off the unicorn charm. "That's awfully pretty. Can I hold it?"

"Not yet," Cressida said. "But you can have it to keep if you help me."

"It's a deal," Drusilla and Drudwyn said at once.

Relief washed over Cressida. "Follow me!" she said, and she put the unicorn necklace in her pocket, picked up the quail roost, and walked as fast as she could toward the flower garden.

Chapter Seven

Cressida returned to the flower garden to discover the quail had already finished eating Bloom's birthday cake and ice cream. A handful gathered around the nearly empty fruit troughs wearing smashed roinkleberries on their heads. Others had pushed pieces of froyananas onto their beaks so they looked like they had long, magenta-and-violet-striped noses. The rest of the quail milled around, hunting for more food. Worthington, Wilhelmina, and Wallaby nervously hid in an empty flowerpot behind Bloom.

Cressida put the quail roost down against the flower garden wall, right in front of one of the fruit troughs.

"What is that?" Bloom asked.

"A quail roost," Cressida explained.

Bloom raised her eyebrows. "A *roost*? We're trying to get the quail to leave the Enchanted Garden, not to stay and sleep here!"

Cressida smiled mysteriously. "I have a plan!" she said. Then she looked into the flowerpot at the worms. "I hate to ask you this," she said, "but could you squirm up onto that quail roost for just a few minutes?"

"But the quail will see us," Wallaby said.

"And they'll eat us," Worthington added.

"I promise to pick you up just as soon as the quail get near you," Cressida said. She wasn't sure what it would feel like to touch the worms, but she wasn't afraid of a little sliminess.

The worms whispered together. "It's a deal," Wilhelmina said.

"Great!" Cressida said. "I promise you'll be safe."

Next, she looked at Drusilla and Drud-wyn, now lying half-asleep at the foot of the quail roost. Cressida pulled the unicorn charm from her pocket and dangled it in front of the mini-dragons. They bolted upright. Drusilla grasped for the charm with her claws, but Cressida kept it out of reach. "When I say *Up!* I need you to fly with this roost over the garden wall and set it down gently in the woods surrounding the Enchanted Garden. The farther you take it from here, the better. As soon as you do that, I promise I'll give you this necklace."

The dragons nodded eagerly.

Cressida turned to Bloom. "Once all the quail are on the roost, can you keep them from jumping off while I rescue Wilhelmina, Worthington, and Wallaby?"

"Absolutely!" Bloom replied.

Cressida looked at the three worms. "Go ahead!" she said. Wilhelmina, Wallaby, and Worthington glanced nervously at each other. Then they wiggled up to the top of the quail roost. Immediately, the entire flock of quail noticed. For a moment, they all cocked their heads, stared at the worms, and blinked. Then the birds shrieked, "*Meep! Meep! Meep! Meep!*" as they charged toward the roost. Soon they began hopping onto the roost's shelves, hunting for the worms.

At just the moment when all the quail had gathered on the roost, one of the quail pecked dangerously close to the worms.

Cressida scooped up the three worms. They were cool and slimy in her hand, but she didn't mind.

At that same moment, Bloom pointed her horn at the trough that sat right in front of the roost. The emerald on her necklace glittered. And then a green stream of sparkling light shot from her horn, making the trough grow so large it created a wall that pressed it up against the roost. Now, the quail couldn't hop off.

"Perfect!" Cressida said. Then she turned to the mini-dragons. "Up!" she called out as she used her other hand to dangle the unicorn charm in front of Drusilla and Drudwyn. The mini-dragons grabbed the roost in their long, sharp claws. They extended their yellow wings. And they soared up into the sky with the roost, and all the quail on it.

Bloom let out a sigh of relief. "I was terrified they were going to eat my entire garden," she said. "Thank you, Cressida."

"Yes," the worms said in unison, "thank you."

"I'm so glad I could help," Cressida said.

Just then, Drusilla and Drudwyn returned and landed in front of Cressida. Cressida sighed as she dropped the necklace Daphne had given her into Drusilla's scaly hands before the two mini-dragons scurried away. She hoped she could save up enough allowance money to buy herself a new one.

That was when Cressida heard Bloom sniffle. She turned and saw the unicorn crying as she looked at all the popped balloons, cake crumbs, puddles of melted ice cream, half-eaten pieces of fruit, and tangled streamers. There were even quite a few quail eggs Cressida hadn't noticed before.

"I'm so sad," Bloom said, "that those quail ruined my garden ball. And now my sisters will still think I'm not capable of planning ahead."

"I'm so sorry," Cressida said, and she wrapped her arms around Bloom's neck.

For a moment, Bloom nuzzled her face against Cressida's. And then she said, "Thank you so much for your help. Right now, I need to be alone for a little while. Will you do me a huge favor and run back to the palace and tell my sisters the party is canceled?"

"Of course," Cressida said. She certainly understood what it felt like to want to be alone. Once, when she hadn't won a prize at her school's science fair, she had been so disappointed that she had wanted to just lie on her bed by herself with the door closed. And another time, when her soccer team lost, she had taken a long walk in the woods by herself.

"Thank you," Bloom said, blinking back more tears. "I'll meet you at the palace soon. I just need a little time to myself first. But please don't go back to the human world without saying good-bye."

Cressida gave Bloom a final squeeze. And then she ran through the vegetable garden, jumping over a pile of sleeping mini-dragons on her way, and then through the orchard, where she waved to Gnorbert and Gnatasha. She felt terrible for Bloom, who had seemed so disappointed and sad.

But as Cressida left the Enchanted Garden's front gate and jogged along the paths leading to the palace, she had an idea: What if she could convince the other unicorns to throw a surprise party for Bloom? It was probably too late to organize another garden ball, but maybe, if they hurried, they could have the birthday celebration ready by the time Bloom returned. Filled with excitement and hope, Cressida began to sprint.

Chapter Eight

Cressida bounded along the clear stones that led to the front entrance of Spiral Palace and burst through the door. As soon as she stepped into the front hall, she heard Prism say, "I'm not going! She didn't even invite me."

All the unicorn princesses except Bloom were standing in a tight circle on the far side of the room. They hadn't heard Cressida come inside.

"I'm positive Bloom meant to invite you," Flash said. "You're her best friend. Something must have happened to your invitation."

Prism stamped her purple hoof. "How many times do I have to tell you? I'm not going."

"I'm staying here with Prism," Sunbeam said.

"Me too," Firefly and Moon said in unison.

Breeze sighed and looked at Prism. "I agree with Flash. Bloom probably dropped your invitation by mistake or accidentally gave it to an off-duty mail-snail."

"She did it on purpose," Prism said, stamping her hoof even harder. "She didn't invite me. I'm not going."

Just then, Cressida sneezed. The unicorns turned toward her.

"I hope you'll excuse us," Flash said. "We were about to leave for Bloom's birthday party, but we're having a disagreement."

"I completely understand," said Cressida, still catching her breath. "But here's the thing. The garden ball has been canceled." Cressida recounted the story of the quail that ruined Bloom's cake, ice cream, fruit, and decorations. She made sure to mention that Bloom had spent weeks planning and preparing for the garden ball.

"I was hoping we could quickly throw together a surprise party for Bloom right now. If we all hurry, we could have it ready by the time she gets back to the palace."

"Great idea!" Flash said.

Breeze nodded.

But Prism shook her head. "No way!" she snapped. "I'm not helping."

"Neither am I," Moon, Firefly, and Sunbeam said.

Cressida's heart sank. By the time she persuaded Prism, Sunbeam, Moon, and Firefly to help with the surprise party, Bloom would probably be back. Then, out of the corner of her eye, Cressida saw something green and glittery fluttering outside the far window. "Just a second!" she said. She hurried out the front door, jogged halfway around the palace, and found what she had spied through the window: an envelope with wings so tiny it could only fly very slowly. The envelope hovered a foot above her head, and Cressida jumped up and grabbed it. She turned it over and read the front:

To My Sister and Best Friend,
Princess Prism

Cressida grinned. She ran back around the palace, through the front door, and over to Prism. "Look!" she said. "Here's your invitation! It looks like Bloom wanted to have it fly to you as a surprise."

Relief, and then joy, spread over Prism's face as she read the words on front of the envelope and then looked inside. "Bloom invited me to her garden ball!" Prism cried out, jumping and dancing across the room. "And I still have my best friend!"

"I told you," said Flash.

"Prism," Cressida said, laughing as Prism spun around on one hoof, "we don't have much time before Bloom comes back. Now that you know she invited you, do you think we could throw a surprise party for her?"

"Definitely!" Prism said. "And I have a great idea! I'm going to gallop back to the Valley of Light to get the rainbow cupcakes I baked this morning and a huge vat of rainbow sherbet I have in the freezer. I was planning on serving them at my next art show, but this is a much better occasion." With that, Prism raced out the palace door.

"I still have some balloons and streamers left over from the Thunder Dash," said Flash. The Thunder Dash was a race Flash hosted every year in the Thunder Peaks. "I'll get them straight away!" She sped off, galloping so fast lightning crackled from her hooves and horn.

"I'm pretty sure I still have some purple party hats back in the Glitter Canyon from a birthday party I threw for the cacti," Sunbeam said. "I'll go find them." Sunbeam, who didn't like to run as much as her sisters, trotted out the front door.

"Here's what I'll do!" Firefly said. "I'll use my magic to create a huge swarm of fireflies. If I spend a few minutes practicing, I bet I can get them to spell out, 'Happy Birthday, Bloom!'" Firefly retreated to the back of the room and began shooting orange light from her horn. Soon, more fireflies than Cressida could count hovered above the unicorn's head.

Breeze thought for a minute. "I've got it!" she said. "I'll go back to the Windy Meadows and get a kite. Cressida, would you be willing to decorate it and write, 'Happy Birthday, Bloom!' on the kite's tail? I'll use my magic so a gust of air flies the kite just over our heads."

"Of course!" Cressida said.

Breeze smiled and hurried out the palace door.

"I know what I can do," Moon said, walking over to one of the front windows. "I'll stand here and wait for Bloom. As soon as I see her coming, I'll use my magic to make the room pitch black. That way, when she walks into the palace and everything is dark, the party will be an even bigger surprise."

👑

Soon, Prism and Flash returned with the cupcakes, the sherbet, two rolls of silver streamers, and a bag of gold balloons. As Prism arranged the cupcakes into a heart in the middle of the floor and Flash blew up balloons, Cressida scooped the rainbow sherbet into a trough and taped the streamers to the walls.

Just as Cressida finished putting up the last streamer, Breeze ran into the front hall with a kite and a bucket of markers. "Sorry

that took me so long!" Breeze exclaimed, panting. "I couldn't find the markers anywhere!"

"No problem!" Cressida said, and she quickly got to work coloring pictures of flowers, fruits, and vegetables on the kite. In bright, colorful letters, she wrote, "Happy Birthday, Bloom! Love, Flash, Sunbeam, Prism, Breeze, Firefly, Moon, and Cressida," on the kite's long tail.

"Well done!" Breeze said, admiring her artwork.

"Thanks!" Cressida said.

Just when Cressida was wondering what else she could do to help get ready for the party, Sunbeam sauntered into the palace with a stack of tall, cone-shaped hats.

Cressida giggled as she fastened a hat to each unicorn's head. Then she put a hat on her own head.

"How do I look?" Sunbeam asked, crossing her eyes to try to see her hat.

"Well," said Cressida, laughing, "to be honest, you and all your sisters look like you have two horns. Does my hat make me look like a unicorn?"

Sunbeam smiled. "Nope," she said. "You just look like a human girl wearing a ridiculous hat."

Right then, Moon called out, "Here comes Bloom! I'll make this room pitch black at the count of three. One! Two! Three!"

Chapter Nine

Suddenly, the front hall of the palace was so dark, Cressida couldn't see her hand when she held it a few inches from her face. She heard the palace door swing open.

"Why is it so dark in here?" Bloom asked, her voice unsteady. "Is everyone gone? Oh, this is the worst birthday ever."

As Bloom began to loudly sniffle, glittery, orange light shot from Firefly's horn, and a swarm of fireflies hovered in the air above her. At first, they looked like a thick cloud of glowing dots, but after a few seconds, they formed the words, "Birthday Happy, Boolm!"

"Oops," whispered Firefly. More orange light streamed from her horn, and then the fireflies spelled out, "Happy Birthday, Bloom!"

"What's going on?" Bloom asked, giggling.

Then, a beam of blue light shone from Breeze's horn. By the fireflies' light, Cressida watched as a gust of wind sent the kite into the air, far enough away from the fireflies that it didn't disturb their birthday message.

"Ready?" Moon whispered. "One! Two! Three!"

Cressida and all the unicorn princesses shouted, "Surprise!" as the lights in the palace came back on.

For several seconds, Bloom looked at the fireflies, the kite, the silver streamers, the gold balloons, the rainbow cupcakes, and the trough of ice cream. Her eyes glittered with delight, and she blinked back tears of happiness. "Thank you!" she said. "Thank you so much! This is absolutely wonderful!"

"It was Cressida's idea," Prism said. "She told us about what happened with the quail. You must have felt disappointed after working so hard to prepare for your garden ball in advance."

Bloom nodded. "I felt pretty awful. But I feel much better now. Also, you all look pretty funny in those hats."

Cressida rushed over to Bloom and wrapped her arms around the unicorn's neck. "Happy birthday," she whispered. Then, she fastened a hat on

Bloom's head and said, "Now you look funny, too!"

Bloom blushed. "I must say, this is the best last-minute party I've ever seen! And trust me, I'm an expert on last-minute parties." Then, Bloom turned to Prism. "Did you get your invitation? I asked Ernest to make it fly to you as a surprise. But when I saw all the quail in my flower garden, I guessed he accidentally cast the wrong spell. I've been so very worried you didn't get your invitation. I didn't want to think I didn't invite my best friend to my birthday garden ball!"

"Well, there was a bit of a mix-up," Prism said. "But Cressida found my invitation and gave it to me. Everything is fine now."

"Phew!" Bloom said.

Prism smiled. "I think it's time for a party game. Bloom, would you like to play Pony, Pony, Unicorn?"

"Yes!" exclaimed Bloom. "That's my favorite game! Come on, Cressida. You'll pick it up in no time." Bloom and the other unicorns formed a tight circle, and Cressida joined them, squeezing between Bloom and Prism.

"I'll go first," Flash said. She began to walk around the outside of the circle, poking each of her sisters with her horn and saying, "Pony!" But when she got to Sunbeam, she shouted, "Unicorn!" and bolted forward, running around the circle and taking Sunbeam's place. The game was exactly, Cressida realized, like Duck, Duck, Goose.

"Flash always chooses me because I'm the slowest runner," Sunbeam said, rolling her eyes as she began walking around the circle, poking each unicorn and saying, "Pony." Then, when she got to Cressida, she squealed, "Unicorn!" before she bolted around the circle. Cressida chased after her, but she had only gotten a quarter of the way around the circle before Sunbeam had slid into Cressida's spot between Bloom and Prism.

"I'm going to be on the outside of this circle forever," Cressida said, giggling.

"Unicorns are much faster runners than human girls."

"It's probably not really fair to play Pony, Pony, Unicorn with a human girl," Bloom said, winking at Cressida. "Let's play something else." But then she looked again at the cupcakes, and her eyes widened. "Actually, would any of you mind if we ate those cupcakes and that sherbet now? I'm starving!"

"I'm hungry, too," Prism said. And Flash, Sunbeam, Breeze, Moon, and Firefly all nodded.

The unicorns gathered around the cupcakes and the trough of rainbow sherbet. "Would you like some, Cressida?" Prism asked. "The cupcakes and the sherbet are both froyanana-flavored."

"Um, no thank you," Cressida said, trying not to gag at the memory of the froyanana she had tasted earlier that day.

Bloom winked at Cressida, and then she looked at her sisters, all enthusiastically chewing. "Can you believe Cressida doesn't like froyananas? She took a bite of one and didn't even want to finish it."

"Really?" said Sunbeam, looking surprised.

"Strange," Flash said.

"Humans are just kind of weird!" Prism said.

Cressida laughed. Then, she heard her stomach loudly rumbling. After so much jumping and running that afternoon, she had worked up quite an appetite.

"I heard that!" Bloom said, nodding toward Cressida's stomach. "I know you probably need to go home soon to eat some human food, but I'm so glad you could join me for my birthday. I was sure those quail had ruined everything. But, thanks to you, this has been my favorite birthday ever. It's been even better than a garden ball!"

"No problem," Cressida said. "I'm thrilled I could be here to celebrate with you, too." Cressida's stomach rumbled even more loudly, and Bloom giggled.

Cressida blushed. "It sounds like I'd better go home and eat a snack! Plus, my birthday party was just last week, and I told my mother I would finish writing all my thank-you cards this afternoon."

"Just promise you'll come back soon," Bloom said.

"Of course I will!" Cressida exclaimed, and she said good-bye to Bloom, Flash, Sunbeam, Prism, Breeze, Moon, and Firefly.

"Good-bye, Cressida!" the unicorns all called out. "We already can't wait for your next visit!"

Cressida plunged her hand into the pocket of her purple party dress. Sure enough, there was the key. She wrapped both hands around the crystal handle and closed her eyes. "Take me home, please!" she said.

Suddenly, the front hall of the palace began to spin, first forming a swirl of pink, white, silver, and purple before everything went pitch black. Then, Cressida felt as though she were flying straight up into the air. She smiled, thinking that the feeling of flying was her favorite part of traveling to and from the Rainbow Realm.

When the flying sensation stopped, she found herself sitting at the base of the giant oak tree. For a minute, the forest spun around her, but then it slowed to a stop. Cressida took a deep breath. She looked down. She was wearing her silver unicorn sneakers, her old jeans with the torn left knee, and her green T-shirt with the red stain on the front. And dangling around her neck on a rainbow ribbon was the unicorn charm Daphne had given her for her birthday. Cressida smiled. Then she stood up and skipped home, her sneakers blinking all the way, to have a snack and finish her thank-you notes.

JOIN CRESSIDA ON HER NEXT MAGICAL ADVENTURE!

TURN THE PAGE FOR A GLIMPSE . . .

Cressida Jenkins followed her older brother, Corey, off the yellow school bus. As soon as his feet hit the ground, Corey raced toward their house. Cressida knew he was in a hurry to play soccer with his friends before he started his homework.

As the bus pulled away, Cressida waved to her friends, Daphne, Eleanor, Owen, and Gillian. They waved back through the bus window, and Gillian shouted, "See you tomorrow, Cressida!"

"See you tomorrow!" Cressida called back. The bus rolled down a hill and disappeared around a corner. Cressida closed her eyes and took a deep breath. She listened to the birds chirping, and smiled as she felt the bright afternoon sun on her head and shoulders. Then, with a grin on her face, she skipped toward her family's house carrying her backpack and four rolled-up pictures she had painted in art class that day. Each was a portrait of one of the unicorns she had met in the Rainbow Realm—a magical world ruled by seven princess unicorns. In one painting, yellow Princess Sunbeam danced among the purple cacti in the Glitter Canyon. In another, silver Princess Flash raced up the Thunder Peaks. A third painting showed green Princess Bloom eating roinkle-berries in the Enchanted Garden. And in the fourth, which she had finished only a few seconds before art class ended, purple Princess Prism posed in front of Spiral Palace, the unicorns' home. She had wanted to paint the other three unicorns—orange Princess Firefly, black Princess Moon, and blue Princess Breeze—but she had run out of time.

"How creative! What a vivid imagination you have," Ms. Carter, her art teacher, had said as she looked at Cressida's paintings.

"Thank you," Cressida replied. She knew better than to tell Ms. Carter, or any other adult, about her trips to the Rainbow Realm. None of the adults she knew even believed in unicorns. They most certainly wouldn't believe Cressida could visit the Rainbow Realm at any time by pushing a special key into a tiny hole in the trunk of an oak tree in the woods behind her house.

Cressida skipped past her neighbors' houses, up her driveway, and along the walkway that led to her family's brick house. All the while, her silver unicorn sneakers' pink lights blinked and flashed. "I'm home!" she called out, as she opened the gray front door.

"Hi, honey!" her mother called from the

living room. Her mother worked from home, and Cressida could hear the sound of typing on the computer.

Cressida carried her backpack and her unicorn paintings into her bedroom and placed them on her bed. In just a few minutes, she planned to start her math homework—a page of long division problems she felt excited to solve. But first, she decided to hang up her paintings. She grabbed a small jar of thumbtacks from her desk. Next, standing on her tiptoes on her desk chair, she tacked each unicorn portrait to her bedroom wall. After she finished, she sat on her bed and thought about her unicorn friends.

Just as Cressida turned to pull her math

folder from her backpack, she heard a high, tinkling noise, like someone playing a triangle. Her heart skipped a beat. She leaped over to her bedside table and opened the drawer. Inside, she found the old-fashioned key the unicorn princesses had given her. Its crystal ball handle pulsed and glowed bright pink—it was the signal the unicorns used to invite her to the Rainbow Realm.

Cressida shoved the key into the pocket of her orange corduroy pants and straightened her yellow T-shirt, which had a glittery picture of a rainbow-striped cat on the front. Then she dashed out of her room, down the hall, and to the kitchen, where she grabbed an apple. "I'm going for a quick walk in the woods!" Cressida called out to her mother. Fortunately, time in the human world froze while Cressida was in the Rainbow Realm, meaning that even if she spent hours with the unicorns, her mother would think she had been gone only a few minutes.

"Have fun, sweetheart," her mother said amid a flurry of typing.

Cressida ran out the back door, through her backyard, and into the woods. As she hurried along the trail that led to the giant oak tree with the magic keyhole, she ate her apple and wondered what the princess unicorns were doing that afternoon. She couldn't wait to see her magical friends, and to tell them all about the pictures she had painted.

But just before she reached the oak tree, Cressida stopped short.

Standing by the tree's trunk stood a unicorn Cressida didn't recognize. The unicorn looked as though she were made of colorless glass. Around her neck hung a ribbon, also clear, with a pendant that looked like a large crystal. In her visits to the Rainbow Realm, Cressida had never met a clear unicorn. And the other unicorns hadn't mentioned another sister.

For a moment, Cressida watched the unicorn, who was frowning as she stared at her transparent hooves.

"Hello," Cressida said, smiling.

The unicorn looked up, startled. Then her eyes lit up with relief. "Cressida! I thought you'd never get here!" the unicorn exclaimed. "We've been calling you all day. I got tired of waiting and decided to come find you."

The unicorn's voice sounded familiar to Cressida, but she couldn't imagine how she might have forgotten meeting a clear unicorn. "Have we met before?" she asked, feeling a little rude.

For a second, the unicorn looked hurt and confused. And then she laughed. "Of course you don't recognize me! I'm clear!" she exclaimed. "It's me, Princess Prism."

"Prism!" Cressida said, rushing over and wrapping her arms around the unicorn's neck. She expected Prism to feel hard and cold, like glass, but instead Prism felt warm and soft. "What happened?"

"Well," Prism began, "Ernest was casting spells this morning, and he accidentally drained all the color from me and my domain, the Valley of Light. And my magic amethyst isn't working the right way."

Prism glanced down at the clear stone on her ribbon necklace. All the unicorn princesses had gemstones that gave them unique powers. Prism usually wore a purple amethyst on a green ribbon that allowed her to turn objects any of the colors of the rainbow.

"Watch what happens when I try to use my magic," Prism said. She pointed her horn at Cressida's silver sneakers. The glass-like stone shimmered, and glittery light shot from her horn. Immediately, the sneakers turned clear, so both she and Prism could see Cressida was wearing one orange sock and one pink sock.

Cressida wiggled her toes and giggled. "I guess I should have worn matching socks today," she said.

"If my magic were working, I could fix that for you," Prism said, smiling. But then her face fell. "The worst part about my magic being broken is I can't make art. I've had exactly thirteen ideas for pictures today since my magic broke, and I haven't been able to paint a single one. It's terrible! Every time I've tried to paint, I've accidentally turned something clear."

Cressida nodded sympathetically. Often, while she was riding in the car or sitting at her school desk, she had ideas for stories she wanted to write and pictures she wanted to draw. She didn't like having to wait until later to start her creative projects, either.

"The only way to reverse Ernest's spell is to find the Valley of Light's missing rainbow and use it to repaint my domain," Prism explained. "You're so good at finding things and solving problems that I thought you could help me. So, will you? Please!"

"Of course!" Cressida said.

"Fantastic!" Prism said, turning toward the giant oak tree. "By the way," she said, kneeling as Cressida climbed onto her back, "where were you all day? We've been calling you for hours!"

"School, of course," Cressida said, gripping Prism's clear mane.

"School?" Prism replied, sounding confused. "What on earth is that?"

Cressida smiled. "It's where human girls and boys go all day to learn things. Like math and science and reading and history."

"Huh," said Prism. "I've never heard of that." She used her hoof to riffle through a pile of leaves at the base of the oak tree. "Now, where did I leave my key? Aha, here it is." She used her mouth to pick up an old-fashioned silver key with a crystal ball handle—just like the one Cressida still had in her pocket. The unicorn pushed the key into a hole at the base of the tree. Suddenly, the woods began to spin, so that first they looked like a blur of brown and green before everything went pitch black. Then, Cressida felt as though they were falling through space, and she held on tightly to Prism's mane.

With a gentle *thud*, Cressida and Prism landed in the front hall of Spiral Palace. At first, the room looked like a dizzying swirl of white, silver, pink, and purple. But soon enough, the spinning room slowed to a stop. Cressida grinned to see Sunbeam, Flash, Bloom, Breeze, Moon, and Firefly all lounging on large pink and purple velvet couches.

Emily Bliss lives just down the street from a forest. From her living room window, she can see a big oak tree with a magic keyhole. Like Cressida Jenkins, she knows that unicorns are real.

Sydney Hanson was raised in Minnesota alongside numerous pets and brothers. She has worked for several animation shops, including Nickelodeon and Disney Interactive. In her spare time she enjoys traveling and spending time outside with her adopted brother, a Labrador retriever named Cash. She lives in Los Angeles.

www.sydwiki.tumblr.com

Magic
Animal Rescue
BY E. D. BAKER

When magical creatures need help,
it's Maggie to the rescue!

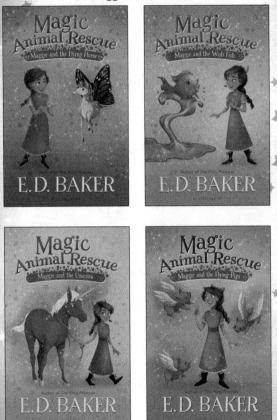

www.bloomsbury.com
Facebook: KidsBloomsbury
Twitter: BloomsburyKids

Princess Ponies

BY CHLOE RYDER

Don't miss Pippa's journey to find the golden horseshoes and save Chevalia!

www.bloomsbury.com
Facebook: KidsBloomsbury
Twitter: BloomsburyKids